ARTEFACT 299

ARTEFACT 299

Accounts of the Zombie Apocalypse

L.A. Binley

Paperback ISBN: 978 1 7399673 1 4
E-Book ISBN : 978 1 7399673 0 7

Cover design by Stone Ridge Books
Edited by N.N. Light Editing Services

Typeset in Garamond

First Edition: October 2021

10 9 8 7 6 5 4 3 2 1

Labinley.com

Day 1

Time becomes meaningless after a while. The passing of days is only noted by the rising and setting of the sun. I guess it really was a human constraint. Even the passing of days is a luxury now. They all blur into one endless loop of running and trying to find a safe space to sleep. Now we're no longer safe, no longer have the luxury to mark the passing of days. I struggle to. It's one of the reasons I made my promise. After everything that's happened, you'd have thought a promise wouldn't be so important. Maybe I struggle to let go of the old ways?

One day, when this is all over and done, someone will read this, and they'll understand. At least I hope they'll understand what we went through. The terror, the sleep deprivation, the real truth of what we suffered through. Always the optimist, Anna, it might get you killed one day. I have to hope. If I run out of hope, why try to carry on living? Why try to survive this?

There's a noise behind me. It doesn't sound safe.

I wish I could go one day without running.

Day 2

I miss electricity. I can't remember how long it's been since I last used it, but I miss it. The artificial lights, the constant connection to the rest of the world. Being able to see without squinting when the sun has gone down. It seemed so natural before, something that would always be there. Maybe if we had more renewable sources, we could have still used them now? I don't know if it would have drawn the hordes quicker, but what I wouldn't do for electricity or central heating! Scratch that, there are some things I wouldn't do. But nostalgia's a bitch when you can't change a single thing.

If you thought this was going to be some sugar-coated reality, you're looking for the wrong thing. Could I make this into a plucky diary of my survival? Maybe? It would be easy to lie. To pretend that I'm not alone every day. To pretend there's some way to survive this. Miss some details here, gloss over some facts there. Fiction would be a nice change to my reality, but that's not the point of this diary. It would be great if everything turned out okay, and all the problems disappeared, but that's not life anymore.

My life is keeping hold of what moves me forward. Like the broken phone in my pocket. I found it on the side of the road, left behind once it was of no use. The screen was smashed, and the battery was flat, but I still picked it up. I wanted to cry, give up and cry. It was stupid really. There's no need for extra weight, especially for something that doesn't do anything, but it reminded me of the past. Something I could keep with me. Maybe it will be a keepsake when the world is back to normal. There are constant reminders of our old lives everywhere. The streetlamps are still there, the cars are abandoned, and there's this phone. Useless and pointless, but oddly reassuring. They have a grounding effect on me. Keeping me going when I feel like giving in.

Day 3

I flicked through the scrawlings and scribbles from the past couple of days. I thought I'd done so much more, put so many more thoughts down and I've not even given you the basics. This has been my reality for such a short while, but it's taken over everything. How are you supposed to introduce yourself in these things? It's not like my old teenage diaries where I used to start everything off with an introduction to myself:

"Hi, I'm Anna Louise Smith. I'm 27 years old. My favourite colour is blue. When I'm older, I hope to be alive. My favourite part about living in North Wales is that I have mountains and coastlines I can visit, but never do."

I may have cringed more than I have ever done before writing that. A small part of me regressed to my younger self, the band tees and ripped skinny jeans calling me from beyond the grave. At least if I could go back, I wouldn't be living through this. I wouldn't be having to try every house I go past to see if I can have safety for a night.

Was this the world anyone imagined? We were told the world was doomed, but never in this way. My thoughts won't concentrate on anything important to share. Maybe next time I will have more ideas to fill the page.

Days 4, 5, and 6

I'm not the best person to have started this. I don't remember to pick up my pen and add in my thoughts. Whoever picks this up will have half-remembered accounts of sleepless nights and fear mixed with bitter attempts at optimism. I hope I'm not the only person to make an account of this outbreak. Outbreak, maybe outbreak isn't the right word, but it feels better than calling it what it is. A zombie apocalypse. At least that's the words I've heard bandied about. I mean, is it really what they are? Even though I'm living through it, I'm still sceptical. Everything I've ever read about zombies has led me to believe they are scientifically impossible. But here I am, in the middle of this zombie outbreak, hoping this day won't be my last.

It seems like everything changed so recently, but it must be at least a couple of months. I don't know if I've managed to move around too much. I don't feel like I've seen that many different places, but I've never stayed in one place for too long. It wouldn't surprise me if I'm doubling back on myself. If that's the case, I'm not too worried about it. If I stay in one similar area, I might be able to bump into someone else. The idea of being truly alone terrifies me. Before this, I didn't mind that I'd chosen my isolated loneliness. I'm starting to realise there's a difference between being alone in a world full of people and being one of the only people alive.

One of the few things I'm thankful for is that I lived in the outskirts when everything happened. Not many people made it out alive. At least the reports in the first couple of days gave the impression that there weren't many survivors. I was one of the last people to leave my small village. It always seemed quiet before, but just before I left, it was like a ghost town. I might have been the last person there. Those who owned a car left quickly, but I'd never been able to afford one. Why would I need it when I could walk to work, and to get food? I've been regretting my thrifty decision though.

Walking to escape has been slow going. I sometimes wish I could stumble across a discarded bike, but who would leave one lying around? If one has been left, someone else has found it before me. I've tried the few abandoned cars, but they're abandoned for a reason. Yeah, the engines turn on, but they don't have any fuel in them. I have tried sweeping through the radio stations. It's what everyone does in the films, don't look at me like that. But there was nothing, no stations were left running, not even Classic FM. There were no amateur broadcasts telling people where to go to survive. There was only static. A dead white noise.

After the first few times, I've stopped trying. There's only so many times you can take your hopes being dashed.

I haven't given up hope entirely. If I was trying to keep people safe, I don't think I'd be interested in setting up a radio broadcast either. I'd want to keep the people with me safe. And if there are people out there, organising somewhere safe to go, it doesn't mean I won't ever run into them.

Day 7

I stumbled across one of them today. It was dead. Or would it be re-dead? Can a zombie truly be dead? Inanimate maybe. All I know is it wasn't moving, and from the looks of it, I'd say it hadn't been moving for a while. I rounded a corner of a small cul-de-sac, and it was there. I jumped. I could feel my heart rate increase, but as I focused on it, I realised it couldn't do anything to hurt me. I zeroed in on the state of its face. Fragments of bones covered in what only looked like ooze. Throwing up wasn't on my list of things to do today, but I couldn't keep it down. The scattered parts and the smell conspired against me. I don't know how I missed the smell before I turned the corner. I wish it had warned me to turn around. I tried not to continue looking at it, but it pulled me in. It could almost make you feel sympathy for it. Almost.

I don't know who managed to kill this one, but I'm thankful. In the short space of time that these have been an issue, I've found that I'm no good at killing them. Even after the past few weeks, I'm still squeamish. If throwing up at the sight of one of them hadn't already given that away. I used to think if the time came, I would be able to do something unpleasant. I'm a disappointment even to myself. Even when it's literally my life hanging in the balance, I can't manage it.

I did try to kill one, right at the start. I had a cricket bat I'd found in someone's shed, and I smacked it over the head. I thought one quick hit would be enough for me to be on my way. I'd managed to sneak up on it from behind and thwack! It didn't have enough force behind it. I went to hit it again, but as it turned around, the mangled mess I'd made of it caused me to throw up. Luckily, I'd been travelling with a couple of other people then. If I hadn't, this diary wouldn't be a thing.

I sometimes wonder what happened to Matt and Kelly. We parted ways before I started writing this diary. It was them who convinced me to start writing it. They were saying how someone should keep a record of what was happening, and then when they'd gone, I stumbled across some notebooks and pens. It seemed like fate. And it gives me someone to talk to. My plan is to find other people, specifically my family. It's why I'm now here on my own, talking to a diary as if it can respond. I could have gone with them, they asked me to, but I need to know that my family is okay. I like to think they're still alive and well somewhere. If I'm surviving, I'm convinced they will be as well.

Days 8 and 9

How have I managed to last this long? I ask myself this all the time. I wouldn't be surprised if you're asking it as well. Honestly? I have no clue. I'm doing better than I ever thought I would. I wasn't one of those people who had a zombie survival plan. Why would I? The likelihood of it happening was slim to none. Even science pointed to it being something that couldn't be done. It seemed like a waste of time, like exercising. There was so much more I could be doing with my time. Why do something that's not necessary and takes time away from other things? I thought my walking every day would be enough to avoid exercise. It's not enough now.

If you'd asked anyone who knew me how likely I would be to last more than a day in an apocalypse situation, most would have said not at all likely. But here I am a few months later. The travel has been slow going. Partially because I'm taking long roundabout ways to go in a straight line. This has helped me so much as I've evaded most of what is out here. It doesn't matter what noise I hear; I try and get out of the way. I know I said I wanted to find other people, but I'm worried I won't be able to trust them. Just because I never had a plan, doesn't mean that I never read any books, or watched any TV shows or films. Humanity never exists in a world like this. A world where people do what's right for the sake of it? I don't know if it's only for the drama, but it's given me a fear of others. I hate not being able to trust people. It makes the sense of isolation even stronger.

It might seem like I'm over-reacting, and maybe I am. A little hysteria never hurt anyone, right? Deep down, I feel it's okay to overreact when you're in an apocalypse-like situation. Maybe it's the only time no one can judge you for it? I still don't want to dwell on it too much. It's easy to spiral when you have no one to keep you grounded. I want to avoid it as much as possible.

Day 10

If I don't make a note of this now, I won't remember to do it. I know that I've already forgotten some of it, but I'm trying to remember all the important parts. This diary is worthless if I don't make important notes.

Earlier today I had the fright of my life, which is saying a lot with how the world has turned upside down. My first few hours walking took me down a secluded area with more trees than usual. The world emitted peaceful energy. My worries were falling from my mind, allowing me to feel free from the horror. I can still feel the breeze caressing my arms. Unfortunately, I had to head further away from the open space as I needed to find somewhere to pee. But my safe spot was apparently not as safe as I thought it was.

I was transported into my very own jump-scare video. I was almost face-to-face with it before I even realised it was there. I still don't know how I managed to sneak up on it. I don't know how I'm alive. My stomach sank, anxiety-induced nausea flooded my body. Luckily, it didn't hear me or smell me. But I don't know how. Maybe their senses aren't as great as we all thought? How are they able to reduce the world to this if they can't find us?

I held back a scream bubbling on my lips and tongue. The world around me stilled, I was a rabbit waiting for the lights to hit. The fear rising through my chest was deafening. I wanted to run, run as fast as I could in the opposite direction, but I couldn't move. I was rooted in place. My fear seeping out and grounding in this one place, an arm's width away from my death. My mind went blank. No thoughts or plans made themselves aware.

I couldn't see anything, or anyone else, around us. Not that I spent much time looking around me, but the zombie didn't seem interested in me at all. Did I not appear as prey anymore? Had I spent so much time fleeing that I had lost my human appearance? I haven't let my mind dwell on what it means too much. The only time I think back to it is to offer thanks. Thanks to whoever is looking out for me and keeping me safe.

Eventually, I felt my limbs unstick. The fear still lingered in my thoughts, but adrenaline won out. I took a small step back, my eyes trained on the decaying form in front of me. One wrong move and I wouldn't be here to tell this story. It never looked toward me. I took another step back. Still, it continued down the road in front of me. I ran. I ran for as long as I could and then I pushed myself to go for even longer. My chest burned, my thighs ached, and I could taste blood at the back of my throat. I pushed myself, not caring about the direction, to make sure I was as far away as possible from what I'd left behind.

I don't think running with wild abandon was my best idea. My supplies are low and I have no idea where I am. Making your way to new cities doesn't help with the disorientated feeling. I like to pretend I know what I'm doing. But I am so lost. I don't have a clue where my mum or brother will be, and I don't know if I can stomach cold, tinned food much longer. Think positive Anna, everything will be okay. If you pretend for long enough, you'll forget everything that's changed.

Day 11

I don't know why it's taken me this long to realise, but I have no idea how I'm going to find anyone. Not my family, not random people also looking for safety. I don't know where I'm going. My sense of direction has never been great, and I've never owned a compass or a map. It's why it's taking me so long to get anywhere. The past few days I've tried to increase my speed. I think I've gone further than I have before. I'm further down a motorway than I was before, but I'm not sure if this was the best route to take. I feel so lost, and I can't even sit and cry about it as it will give me less of a chance of getting out of this situation. I want to wallow in the rubbish life I've found myself in. My hope of finding my family is slowly dwindling. Disappearing into that place where all my hopes for life have gone in the past few months. I can't work out where they will have gone to, and I think heading to their houses will be pointless. They won't have waited around.

Why hadn't I done some sort of survival course? Oh yeah, because this was the last thing from my mind. It's this what-if thinking I need to break out of. I can't change how I lived my life; I can only change how I continue to live. I need to focus on a way to survive. If I can get through this then there is a very, very, very slim chance I might be able to see one of them again. But I'm going to need to figure out where I am, and where I'm going first. Maybe I'll hit a road sign and I'll know the places it mentions.

My sprint yesterday may have caused me more issues than I thought it would. My only thought was to get as far away from it as I could. I'm sure anyone would have done the same. I'm not sure running wildly in a place I'm not familiar with was a great plan. I thought I'd ran in a straight line, but I'm starting to think that's not the case. I left behind the ruins of the little suburbia and headed to the wilds. Well less wilds, and more uninhabited countryside. I would not be surprised if I've twisted round and I'm now going back on myself.

I'm worried about where I am as my food supplies are running low. Lower than I assumed they were. If I take everything into account, I've maybe got enough food to last me the week. Is a week long enough to find more food? Maybe if I'd not run into the middle of nowhere. If I'd learnt anything useful about the countryside, I might know what berries or fruits I can eat. Scavenging would be a lot easier. I'm not sure being able to recognise a silver birch will give me much luck. Are they edible? I don't even know. I can't bring myself to hunt anything and eat it. Standing on snails makes me feel sick, never mind having to gut something. Or skin it. I'm shuddering thinking about trying to do it. How have I managed to survive for this long? I don't think I'll ever know.

Day 11
Continued

This diary has become my confidant. I don't know if I'd be able to keep track of anything if I hadn't picked up that pen a few weeks ago. Was it a few weeks? I'm not sure about the days anymore, and sometimes I think I've made a note that day only to realise a few have passed. I've tried to keep this as correct as I can, but it's not an easy task. At least this is keeping me sane, or at least as sane as you can be for these times.

I'd thought my entry for today would be done. I'm nestled in the only cover I could find. Some sparse bushes with some trees overhanging nearby. I don't know how far I've come from the road. It's safer to stop for a few hours at a time before heading off and finding another space to rest. My mind calmed enough to drop the fears and anxieties of travelling. I felt myself drifting off when I heard a noise.

I tried to brush it off, it's easy to mistake a noise.

Or pretend that one noise is another. A slight rustling of leaves could be the wind or some unseen predator. This time was different. It didn't stop. I was sure I'd not heard this sound in a while. Footsteps. I froze. I tried to keep myself as still as possible, worried that any movement would give away my location. Dizziness crashed over my head, my thoughts racing as fast as my heart. The only positive, the one thing my mind had managed to sift through; it didn't sound like a zombie. The footsteps were too regular, none of the usual shuffling and scraping. Another noise filtered through the panic, as soft as a summer breeze, the sound of voices. Whoever was talking was too far away for me to hear the words, but loud enough for the murmurs to reach me. This was not a zombie. The guttural, animalistic noise that follows them around was missing. This sound was almost musical in its conversation. Although it sounded human, I was reluctant to leave my spot.

I know, I know. I said I was going to find some people and join up with them. I was going to find some company so I have more than a diary to keep me sane. But I felt wary, nervous. I've spent so much time alone that I don't know if I can trust anyone that isn't me. What if the calmness of their voices was a lie?

I willed them to walk away and leave me alone with my hiding space. As much as I needed to rest, I couldn't quiet my mind and slow my heart. Not until I felt like no one was going to find me. Tense and on edge, I waited until the sound of people vanished. Leaves rustled next to me. Branches creaked. Nature lived as I strained for their voices. I waited longer than I needed to before wriggling into a more comfortable position. I thanked whatever was watching over me that they hadn't noticed where I'd crawled. Small mercies, eh?

It's taken me a long time to feel relaxed enough for me to be able to get any sort of proper rest. The unsettled feeling in my stomach refusing to budge. It's weird. That was my first time in the presence of real, living people in weeks. And yet I hid. Maybe I am more of a coward than I thought I was. No, I know I can trust myself. I have to trust my gut instinct. If there wasn't a reason to stay hidden, I might have given up my only chance to travel with someone else.

I dozed a little with my diary in my hand. I'm surprised it's not covered in dirt and mud. I've never been good at keeping them safe. It seems a little odd that the only time I can keep a diary going and keep the diary safe is when I'm running for my life. I don't know what I'd have done if someone had come across me. What if I'd have dropped this? Would I have looked for another one? Or would I have taken it as a sign to give up?

I think the earlier fear is getting to me. I feel on edge and jittery. I want to feel safe and relaxed. Is that too far into the past to happen again? There's been too much adrenaline rushing over me the past couple of days. It might be something I can get used to. This jittery, fluttery feeling consumes me. It's too much to hope everything will go back to normal, but a girl can dream. Right?

Days 12 and 13

I let my guard down too much yesterday. It was the first time in a long while I've given myself any time to feel free. I felt relaxed and at peace until they snuck up on me. I'm not sure where I wandered to, but I found some running water. I didn't risk drinking any of it, and it was freezing, but I've never felt more alive than the quick rinse I took. It made me feel like the old Anna for a short while. While I seized my opportunity, so did they.

I'd stupidly left my bag and bat on the edge of the stream. Or maybe it was a river. Whatever it was, I'd waded out too far. The cold water splashed across my face as rocks clinked behind me. I span around in time to see someone snatch up my bag. The other threw whatever they could wrap their hands around.

"Hey, give that back," I shouted as I pushed myself back towards my possessions. "If you're looking for food, you've stumbled across the wrong person." I continued my way towards them as I ducked beneath the barrage of rocks, stones, and twigs being thrown my way.

The girl, who had my bag in her hands, darted backwards as I scrambled up the side of the embankment. "Seriously, you're wasting your time."

"Why would we listen to you? Course you don't want us to take anything." She said, rummaging inside the rucksack. "Look, we only need a little bit, you can have the bag back."

I tried moving closer to her but forgot about her partner in crime. They continued to throw whatever they could at me. I scowled at the boy. Since I'd left the water, he'd looked for larger objects to try and keep me away.

"Fine, don't trust me. But I'm almost out of food myself. There are only the things I don't want to eat anymore. Enjoy the sardines."

"What? That's all you have?" The girl pushed the bag away from her face as it scrunched up, but she had seen for herself. I wasn't lying. She threw the bag towards me. "I think we'll pass. C'mon Daniel. Might as well look somewhere else for food."

Daniel slowed his missiles. "You sure, Rachel? I don't mind eating sardines."

"You honestly disgust me sometimes." She shuddered. "But, I'm sure." She said retreating.

Daniel took a few steps back to catch up with her before he completely stopped his attack on me.

"Sorry, my wares couldn't have been more appetising for you." I shouted at them. My hands scrunched by my sides at the mess the girl, Rachel had left. As if it wasn't difficult enough trying to survive at the moment, but now I have to repack what was littered in front of me.

The tell-tale prickle in my eyes made me press my palms into them. I wouldn't let myself break, not over something so small. It might not look like a lot, this bag with the few tins of food, but this is all I have in the world. I took a deep breath and decided. I don't know what it was that made me do it, maybe it was the loneliness I'd been feeling. Sadness trickle over me as I watched them go. I swung my closed bag over my shoulder and grabbed the cricket bat.

"Hey, you two, wait up."

They both stopped, turning to face me.

"It may seem daft, as you've just tried to steal from me, but would you like to travel together? I know you don't have a clue who I am, and you might not trust me. But I've been walking around for weeks on my own and I could do with some company."

"You want us to travel with you?" Rachel looked at me in disbelief. "You don't know who we are, and you want us to come with you?"

"Honestly, with how the world has turned out I don't mind who you are. I think travelling in a group might be better than travelling alone. Look, I know you have each other but you don't seem to be doing so well on your own. We could help each other out."

Rachel and Daniel looked at each other and began whispering. I couldn't make out what they were saying. Daniel had pulled them back a few steps, to keep me out of earshot. The hand gestures and scrunched up faces weren't giving me much hope. They didn't know me, and they didn't know if they could trust me. It's how I was feeling a couple of days ago. For all they knew, I could be trying to trick them. The fear of what the world had become plagued my thoughts, so why not theirs.

After a tense few minutes, Daniel looked at me. His brown eyes narrowed. "You can join us."

Rachel elbowed the boy, glaring at him before turning to look at me. "What he meant to say was thanks for offering to help us out. And we're sorry about trying to steal your bag."

"As long as you don't try to take my things again, we're fine." I spoke. "Companions?"

I held out my hand.

Rachel cleared the short distance to shake it. "Companions."

Day 14

"How did you two start travelling together?" I asked them as we set off this morning.

"We were on a school trip together. We were," Rachel took a deep breath. "We were heading back to the coach when we saw this person trying to get on. He didn't look right. His face didn't look right. There was something wrong with it. I was drawn in. At least until the screaming started."

"We were at the start of the crowd. We could escape." Daniel added.

"Yeah, if we'd hung back, I don't know—" Rachel's brown eyes became distant. "There was so much blood." She whispered. "I don't know how many people were able to get away. Danny pulled my arm and we ran. I didn't look back."

"At least you made it out of there." I smiled weakly.

"I suppose so."

"It was good of you to stick together, have you

been friends for long?"

The mood lifted as Daniel and Rachel began laughing. I glanced between them, unsure what joke I'd made.

"I always said you didn't need to worry." Daniel said as he ruffled Rachel's mousy brown hair.

"I've told you not to do that." She muttered, trying to fix the mess he'd made. "Daniel likes to remind me he's the older brother, but it was only four minutes. It's not like that counts."

"If it didn't count, it wouldn't annoy you so much." His smile was infectious.

Rachel glared at him as she continued walking.

"At least you get to travel with some family, and you know you're both okay." I said to them.

Rachel became pensive. "I'm glad Danny's safe, and we're together but I'd love to find Mum and Dad. We headed home but we couldn't find them; it did take us a while though as we got lost a few times. We'd hoped they waited for us." She dropped her head, her hair hiding her face from view. "But they might not have thought we made it back. I can't blame them for going, but I'd love to find them one day."

"What have I said, Rach?" Daniel said softly. "We can't dwell. They didn't leave a note behind, and we don't know where they went."

"Aren't you worried about what might have happened to them?" I asked him.

He shrugged. "Sometimes, not really. I want them to be alive. But I've come to terms with this reality now. I doubt I'll ever see them again. Not unless something happens to stop this."

"Doesn't it bother you?"

"If I don't think about it, it doesn't matter, you know? We'll either find them or we won't."

His nonchalance was disconcerting. I couldn't tell if he meant it, or if he was trying to detach himself from what was happening.

"I wish I could shut myself off as well as you, Dan." Rachel said. "I try not to dwell. I've noticed the more I do, the more it starts to hurt." She took a deep breath. "Sorry, I wish I could see them one last time. I miss my mum," she laughed slightly to herself. "I know everyone probably says the same, but I wish I'd told her I loved her the day we left. Instead, I ran out the door chucking a goodbye over my shoulder. It sucks, that was probably the last time I'll see her."

Rachel's eyes watered as she spoke. I know how she felt in some way, but it must have been worse for her. I'm nearly 30 and I wish I knew what had happened to my family. There were so many times I could have told them I cared. So many missed chances. But how old was Rachel? No older than 17, maybe 18 at a push. Having to deal with that sort of loss must be hard on her. Not even being 20 and your entire family was practically gone must be difficult to deal with. It's not something I'd wish on my worst enemy.

"At least you have Daniel." I said smiling at her.

"Yeah, he's not too bad." She laughed, choking down the tears. "We've been able to keep each other pretty sane. I don't know how you've managed so long on your own! I know there were a few times I would have fallen over the edge if Danny wasn't here."

"There were a few times I wasn't sure I'd pull myself back either." I admitted. "It was easier at the start, travelling with a bunch of people. But I made a decision to go my own way. I've been so focused on trying to find my family. I didn't want anyone to sidetrack me. If I couldn't find them, then I might have to admit I'm all alone. Not that I haven't regretted my decision to go solo at times." I paused as the words tumbled from me. "Sorry, you don't want to hear all that. I didn't realise I'd been holding all that in. That's what I get for being alone for so long." I chuckled. The melancholy falling from me as I changed the subject. "So, how has your tactic of stealing other people's supplies been working for you?"

Both had the dignity to look embarrassed.

"That was the first time we'd tried to." Rachel winced. "We'd finished all our food a couple of days ago and we'd not been able to find anywhere to scavenge from. We are sorry, but it's worked out for all of us."

"We were desperate." Daniel added. "You were distracted, and we didn't think it through."

I chuckled again, relishing in the ability to do so. "It's okay. Desperation could get to us all at some point. We need to find somewhere to grab food soon. I don't think mine will last the three of us for long." I looked pointedly at Rachel, "and yeah we're going to have to eat cold, tinned fish."

Rachel's face scrunched up. It wasn't something I was looking forward to much either, but sometimes beggars can't be choosers. Worry wrapped around me as I checked through what we had left. Maybe two days worth of food? I hope it will be enough to keep us going until we hit some houses with food left inside. Maybe we'll get lucky and find some extra bags or something so Rachel and Daniel can carry their food.

Day 15

We managed it! We found food. Sure, there might not have been a lot of it, and we couldn't find any extra bags to use, but we have enough to last us a few more days. If I've worked it all out right. Coming across the outcroppings of houses isn't too difficult. Finding any food left in them is the main struggle.

I feel giddy at this small accomplishment. Not only am I keeping myself alive, but I'm also helping two other people as well. I've never felt like this before. I'm on a high. Calm down, Anna. There's more you need to do if you want to make sure all three of us survive. My emotions flip-flop between euphoria and cynicism. This is only one small step to keep us going. There are so many other things we need to do. I feel guilty celebrating the small stuff. Have I done anything to validate it? Never mind, that's a thought to analyse another day.

Okay, so the food offerings were minimal, but we grabbed some tinned fruit, tinned vegetables, and instant noodles. Do heat and fire attract zombies? I don't know, but even if I can't warm them up, the seasoning packet will help make some of the other foods taste better. Do I want to eat dry noodles? Will Rachel or Daniel want to eat dry noodles? I guess it will be better than nothing in a pinch. Adjusting to this new diet is challenging to say the least. It is either adjust to eating the weird, cold mess or starve. Luckily, my survival instincts haven't completely left me.

On the plus side, calorie intakes are reduced by a hell of a lot in an apocalypse. Yeah, it's mainly processed or at least over-preserved tinned goods but it's probably better than I was eating this time last year. What I wouldn't give for a freshly baked baguette and a slab of butter though. Something I used to take for granted, gone forever. My diet might be dubiously better, but my life expectancy has reduced by around 40 years. You win some, you lose some.

Rachel and Daniel have been quiet for the past day. I don't know if it's because they don't really know me, or if they are like that. They keep an eye out for each other though. Are they even aware of the way their eyes flick to find their twin at some unseen noise? Maybe, maybe not. It's strengthened my resolve to do what I can to find my family. I might not be alone anymore, but I can't let myself forget them. I wonder if my brother ever managed to hole up in a gym like he always said he would.

Days 16, 17, and 18

Daily updates are not my forte. Am I the person who should be trying to record what's going on? Even missing some days, I think I've done a good job. Honestly, time doesn't seem to be registering much anymore. Even with Rachel and Daniel joining me, days aren't standing out. The world and surviving are falling into one long blur of abandoned villages, towns, and cities. We don't rest for long, but we stop often. This is the main problem. We don't have set times to show the passing of the day. A break is called by any of us when we are feeling like we need some time to stop.

"Where are we going?" Rachel asked.

I pushed myself into the groove of the tree we were resting by. "I'm not sure. I was aiming for Bournemouth to see if I could find my mum and brother. But I'm starting to think they won't be there anymore, and I don't know where else to look." My body tensed, waiting for the pain to wash over it.

Her arm reached across to comfort me. "We'll help you look for them." She stared earnestly at me. "I promise."

"Thank you." I whispered. I didn't trust myself to speak louder. I could already feel my voice breaking. "Aren't you going to look for your family though?"

Rachel shrugged. "We already went home and they didn't tell us where they were going. They might not have made it out of there at all. I don't want you to feel like you don't have anyone. At least I have Daniel to annoy me."

"What are you two conspiring about?" Daniel asked as he flopped down between us.

"We're going to help Anna look for her family." Rachel beamed at him. "She needs someone other than us two."

Daniel began to groan but Rachel kicked his outstretched arm. "No, none of that. What else are we going to do?"

"Find a safe haven."

She scoffed. "We don't even know that's real."

"You mean there's a real safe haven?" I asked. "You were looking for a real place."

Daniel rubbed the mark on his arm. "Maybe. I'm just assuming. Some people might have built up a secure location. If they have, we'll find it."

His eyes flared with the conviction of this haven being something tangible. My hope rose with that look. The possibility of somewhere safe to go. Somewhere where we might survive this? I couldn't help sinking into that feeling of warmth and comfort. But reality soon set in. How many radios had I turned on only to hear static? If there was a haven, wouldn't they have tried to send out word somehow? The UK isn't that big, it couldn't be too difficult to let people know. My lips parted, the cynicism ready to leap out and squash his hope. I stopped them. What right did I have to cut someone down like that?

"We can all try and find it together." I heard my voice, more strained than it had been minutes before.

Daniel looked at me. His hope was still there, but there was also confusion swirled and muddying his eyes. "Even if we can't find your family, you can help us look for it."

I've been struggling to get over his hope all day. His belief in finding somewhere safe seemed almost childlike. Was it holding onto something like that which was pushing him forward each day? Is that what it looked like to want to survive this? Is that why I am struggling to keep going?

Day 19

All thoughts of a haven have been pushed from our thoughts today. Our food supplies are low, and we've been wandering too close to a motorway for too many days. I don't know how far I am from where I started, from where I lived for the past few years. It is probably a lot further than I could guess at. Miles of walking, and now I'm going to let us starve because I don't know which way to stray from this road.

I've been distant today. I don't know if it's the realisation that I have no idea what I'm doing, or if it's the darkness that has started to linger at the edges of my thoughts. I'm struggling more and more to keep my optimism up and now I feel like I have to force it out. Travelling on my own meant I didn't have to worry about people talking to me, or asking me questions. Now, I don't feel that I can be myself without causing them to worry. I need to be strong. I'm only 27, not much older, but I have this feeling that I need to be strong for them. I need them to know that this is something we can get through.

I wish I could steal some of Daniel's faith. Even with a small sliver of it, I could ward this off. Ward off whatever this darkness is that wants to dominate me.

Day 19 Cont.

Say what you want about power naps, but they help. I've read through my thoughts from earlier today and almost ripped the page out. What was going through my mind? Although I've left it now, I'm still tempted to get rid of it. My fingers twitch, waiting for the command to pull the page from the seam and throw it into the grass. I'll resist. I said I would be truthful here, give a full representation. I suppose I should be happy it's the first time I've fallen so low. Don't get me wrong, despair is eating at my thoughts. Reminding me that we still don't have enough food to last longer than a day at most.

I pulled us from the road. I wanted to find somewhere I could sit quietly, without too much worry, and I wanted to see if I could find our way back to the ruins of civilisation. I don't know what god, or goddess, of luck is smiling down on me. Or maybe it's not me, but I will be sending up thanks for as long as I survive this.

I stumbled us into a retail park. Eerie is probably not explaining it enough, but it felt creepy. I'd have to guess it was around midday, maybe a little later. All the shops had been left with all their shutters up.

"Let's see if there's anything left worth taking from here." I whispered to the twins.

They nodded before falling in step behind me. Rachel closed the distance between her and her brother until they were almost touching. What I wouldn't give for that feeling of safety. We headed for the discount shop first, they used to sell food. If we were lucky, there might still be something we could take.

The harsh metal of the door sent tingles through my body. The cold seeping through my fingers. I pulled my jacket down to bury my palms and shoved against the door with my covered shoulders. The stagnant air swirled around us. The area was still, quiet.

"How long do you think it's been since anyone was in here?" Daniel asked as he plucked his way through the ransacked mess.

My fingertips skimmed across the top of a shelf. The dust felt furry, but it hadn't reached the grimy stage. The stage where the grease covered you as well. "Maybe a month. Hopefully, long enough that's it's safe."

After so long hiding from civilisation, walking into a shop felt weirdly normal. Okay, having to sidestep over discarded items and trashed shelves wasn't normal. It might have even hit home how doomsday-esque the world was, but it gave me an odd comfort. Like the broken mobile phone snug in my pocket.

"These could be useful." Rachel said as she picked up a couple of bags. She dusted them down eyeing them over for any breaks. "What d'you think, Anna?"

She thrust the bags in my direction. I didn't spend much time looking over them. They would be fine for what we needed them for. "They look perfect. We might struggle to get much in them, but between us, we should be able to last longer between food trips."

Rachel beamed at me, slinging one of the bags over her shoulder before heading up to Daniel.

I scanned the shelves. As I thought, there wasn't much that we'd be able to take from here. I picked up the packets of jelly, noodles, anything that might not be the most nutritious but would keep us going. I stopped my pacing through the shop. My eyes mesmerised by the item strewn along the floor. Face wipes. Unopened packets of face wipes. My vision blurred as I reached out to pick one up. I wiped the tears on the back of my arm. How long had it been since I'd been able to clean any of the grime off my face? Too long. They would take up some space I might need for food, but a couple of packets might be the luxury I needed to keep me going.

"You found anything?" I asked Rachel and Daniel as I caught up to them.

"Apart from the bags, not much." Rachel responded.

"This blanket." Daniel said holding it out. "With it being the end of September, we might want something to keep us warm when we rest."

"I'd not thought of that, good thinking. Were there any more of them?"

He shrugged at me as he stuffed it into the bag Rachel had given him.

"I'll have a look. It's not an obvious thing to take."

"Okay." I turned to Daniel. "Want to help me find some food?"

"Sure, I guess."

"We might as well find something that you'd want."

I headed down another aisle, hoping Daniel was following. Rachel had opened up to me easily, but Daniel was more reluctant. I didn't want to overstep. Not everyone would want to open up with worry and death around the corner. It wouldn't stop me from trying to get to know him. If we could speak to the people we were travelling with, we might as well travel alone.

"I hope chocolate wasn't on your list. These shelves don't look like they've been filled for a while."

"I'm not much of a sweet tooth. Rachel might be disappointed."

"Do you think cocoa powder would help?" I said grabbing a tin.

I turned to see Daniel pulling a face, "what would you use that with?"

"Water? On its own?" I glanced at the label. "Not baking, that's for sure. It might hit a spot."

He didn't look convinced, but he took the tin from me and placed it in his bag.

"Do you think we'll be able to survive this?" He asked quietly.

I paused. Is it okay to lie to children, well teenagers, in an apocalypse? "I don't know. I try not to get my hopes up, but if I give in then I know I won't survive. I have to push myself to keep living. Finding my family, or some traces of them helps." I smiled at him. "But knowing I have to look out for you two helps as well."

"I'm guessing you've never had to comfort someone before?"

"Was it that bad?"

"Not the greatest, Anna." He smiled wryly. "But with this, I guess it was better than nothing. Thanks for at least being honest."

"Any time. Now, let's see if there are any other weird things we can eat?"

Day 20

It might not have been a bed, but sleeping with four walls surrounding you has been something I'd forgotten. We decided to set up a mini-camp in the shop. Don't worry, we barricaded the doors so we would at least be alerted if anything tried to get in through the front. I don't think I've felt so refreshed in a long while. No wind whistling past my ear. No unbroken sleep from crunches and crackles from the world around us. Today feels like a better day. A day where hope might be able to pull us through.

Day 20 Cont.

Why *do my bouts* of optimism always end up short-lived? I wonder if the universe can sense it? "Oh, it looks like Anna might be feeling too good about the state of the world, here you go. A nice little present to remind yourself of how things work now." We'd not long set off out on our quest to Bournemouth when Daniel stilled.

"Did you hear that?"

I shuck my head as Rachel edged closer to him. He cocked his head to one side.

"I'm sure there was something, but maybe." He paused, his eyes distant. "No, I must have been imagining it."

"Let's be careful anyway."

They nodded at me before continuing. After a few more steps, I heard it. A low rumbling growl vibrated through my body. I fell still. Rachel's eyes widened and Daniel pushed his hand over her face. I slowly turned to face the way we came. The path behind us seemed empty, but there was no mistaking the noise. I motioned for the twins to carry on as I pulled the bat from behind my back. Would I be able to use this properly? Maybe not, I thought, but it would be better than nothing. I drifted behind them, keeping watch around me.

The nerves shook my hands. Fear seeping into every step I took. The growl rumbled again. I spun on my heel and spotted the lumbering figure. It lurched forward, unsure of itself. If we ran, would we be able to get out of the way? Would it follow us? Or would it give us the time we needed to get away?

I jogged, catching up to Rachel and Daniel within a few seconds.

"It's behind us." I whispered, jabbing back the way we'd came. "We can run, you two go first and I'll keep an eye on it following us."

"Are, are you sure?" Rachel whispered. "What if we lose you?"

"Don't worry, there's something off about this one. I'm not sure what, but it doesn't seem as focused. Trust me, I'll catch up with you when I can."

"Okay," Daniel said as he grabbed Rachel's hand. "We'll see you soon."

I turned my back on them as they sped off. The zombie paused at the sudden noise, but it didn't pick up any pace. I backed away from it, heading in the same direction as the twins but keeping my eye on the danger behind us. Its feet scuffed the floor as it shuffled along. The clothes it had died in were torn and shredded like every other one I'd seen. You'd think there was a class on how to perfect the zombie dress code. As I continued my journey back, I noticed something.

There wasn't as much dirt on this one. Or at least the clothes didn't look to be in as much of a need of a clean. I don't know what that means.

When I was sure the zombie wouldn't chase after us, I turned and ran in the direction Daniel had pulled Rachel. Hopefully, they wouldn't have been able to get too far without me.

Days 21, 22, 23, and 24

Even keeping an eye on two other people hasn't upped what I can talk about. Ever since the encounter last week, my coward levels have spiked. Sure, I could mention I've barely slept for the past few days, or the worsening condition of my breakfast as I try to ration my food, or mention how the weather is slowly turning worse. Those are my reality, but is it the reality I should be sharing? Aren't apocalypses supposed to be recorded by the perky, feisty protagonists? Every day that passes, I feel like I'm not the one who should be doing this. I've almost thrown this diary away so many times. If only I could bring myself to do it one day. To give up. To not be burdened with this choice I've made.

Alright, Anna you've had your moment of sorrow. Don't wallow too much.

I should be showing how society has collapsed. How the world broke all around us. We watched it fracture and split. There was nothing we could do to stop it. Nothing we can do now to stick it back together. The problem was the panic. As soon as the panic set in, and the fear began to spread, society collapsed completely. There's nothing left to show of civilisation except ransacked houses, and abandoned cars. The ruins of the modern era. Maybe hundreds of years from now, when we deal with the danger in front of us, tourists will come here to see what the world was once like.

As we walk, I keep these thoughts to myself. Let them churn and twist through my mind. It is not the happy type of conversation I think a couple of teenagers want to have. Does anyone want to be confronted with an idea so bleak? They both seem so young, they should be thinking about how they will spend the rest of their lives. Not worrying if their lives will only last until tomorrow. It's why I don't want to make it harder on them.

We've rested more than usual since the zombie coming after us the other day. It seems counter-intuitive. Stay in one place for longer than you usually would. I'm still reasoning it out myself. Rachel argued for it.

"I don't think we're rested enough to escape them." She mentioned as we walked.

"What do you mean?" I asked.

"If Danny hadn't been pulling me along, I wouldn't have gotten out of there. I don't know if it's not having enough rest, or if it's the lack of food. But I'm worried. What if it had been closer?" Her eyebrows drew together, scrunching up her face.

"We would have made it." I said, forcing the optimism into my words. "Or at least, I'd have helped you two get far enough away."

"That's not what I mean. No one should have to sacrifice themselves to keep the others safe. We need to get stronger. We need to be less tired. I don't want to lose anyone else."

"I agree with Rachel. We all need to find a way to survive this, or at least find a way to not use one of us as bait."

"We could take longer rest breaks. But unless one of you knows how to catch an animal and turn it into food, or which berries aren't poisonous, I don't think there's much we can do about that."

"I think you can eat acorns." Rachel volunteered. "But they might not taste the greatest. And I'm not sure if you need to cook them first." Her voice trailed off as her mind tried to find the information.

"It's a start." I smiled encouragingly at her. "So, what are you suggesting? How long should we give it between rests? I'm not going to lie, I prefer to be moving. I hate the stillness of sitting and waiting around, but I know when I'm outvoted."

"Maybe we try doing hour and a half rest stops, or as close to as we can guess?" Daniel said. "If we do that five or six times, we might feel better. What would that be? Around eight hours. Not quite the prescribed amount of sleep."

I nodded. "Good idea. I still dislike the overall plan, but if we're able to move around and find new places to rest, it might work out better. Want to start now?"

Rachel and Daniel looked around themselves. The road we were on was open. Too open to find anywhere to rest without someone, or something, being able to see us.

"Okay, maybe we could find somewhere to give us some shelter first."

"Shelter sounds like the better option."

It didn't take long to stumble across an estate. The detour will take us some time to make up, but it also gives us somewhere to hide. I let Rachel and Daniel find somewhere to bunker down while I searched the building. A few packets of bandages and half-empty boxes of painkillers were all I managed to ferret out. A lucky score in the wilds of the zombie ravaged world.

I don't know what caused these things to come into being, a virus or mutation of a virus maybe. The way they behave doesn't seem natural. Their hearing seems to be so much more impressive than a standard human's. It's why I don't understand how we escaped the other day. How did it not know where we were going? In the past, I'd successfully distracted one of them by throwing a rock in the opposite direction. It had zeroed in on the noise. Was it only something that older zombies learnt? Did that mean they weren't equally deadly? I wouldn't let my thoughts dwell on that. If there was a chance, even a small one, that we could overpower the younger ones, maybe, just maybe, there might be a way out of this.

Day 25

Changing rest tactics is working. My mind no longer drifts and wanders during the day. I'm sharp, alert, focused even. The dark thoughts have retreated under the new regime. I wouldn't say that my thoughts on the apocalypse have flipped 180. There are still those niggling feelings of doubt. Like they would ever disappear completely, that would be too much to ask for. However, I can see a way out. If there are us three, there has to be more people surviving. I refuse to believe we are the only people who have found some way to live. Living might be too strong a word, but you get the idea.

Don't get me wrong, I'm not planning out the day we're rescued. I'm not letting myself get that hopeful. Although I would be a liar if I didn't say I dream of hot food each day, and the softest mattress to sleep on every night. Everyone needs some fantasies to continue, right? I don't know if it's meeting Rachel and Daniel which has caused this shift in my feelings. They haven't done anything, in particular, to make me think that there is anything else to the world now. I just know that I was slowly giving up.

The pressure to keep my spirits up each day isn't weighing me down like it used to. I'm no longer saddled with the weight of surviving on my own. I'm no longer suffocating in despair. Each day felt like a day abandoned at sea, with wave after wave of despair, loneliness and desolation washing over me with its unrelenting force. I was battered and bruised. Now? Now I am going forward. There is still a slight buffeting, but it can't topple me anymore.

Day 26

I don't know how we've managed it, but we can't see any signs of civilisation. How? England's not a huge place and yet we've not been able to find anywhere to rest safely for the past half a day. I'm lost. Correction, we're lost. Hopelessly lost. I'm starting to worry we've been walking in a circle. When we set out, I was certain we would find somewhere soon enough. It's why I said we should venture further away. I didn't realise it would cause an issue. How is there so much space? I'm starting to regret all the time I spent cosied up in my flat. I could have spent that time getting used to hiking and understanding how to stay safe out of the city. I could have at least bought a compass.

Who am I kidding? I could get lost in my own backyard. I might have enjoyed the time outside, but it wouldn't have helped me now. I would still be aimlessly carving out paths in the middle of nowhere. My only solace is I'm not on my own and wandering without direction. Being in a group feels less terrifying. Not that my arms have de-goose bumped since I realised our predicament.

On the plus side, Rachel has remembered a couple of berries that aren't poisonous. Blackberries were her first thought. I know, that's an easy one but my mind has blanked on all ways to forage and stay safe. It's a wonder I've lasted this long. Luckily, they have still been in season. Not enough left to keep us full, but can you even fill up on berries? It's helped eke out the food that we'd picked up, but if we don't find our way back to a village or something, our worries will be more with finding something to eat than being eaten.

Our talking had been at a minimum today. I was still too wired to make any noise, but maybe the twins were trying to save some energy. As much as I'd missed being able to speak out loud to someone, and I don't want to give it up again, I want to keep us as safe as I can. Having someone to speak to other than myself, has done wonders for my train of thought. Nothing has happened to us since the other day, but there are unnatural noises following us. Encircling us. I've not been able to tell where it's coming from. Every noise quickened our pace.

"Do you think that one is from something alive or dead?" Daniel asked.

"Shut up Dan! I don't want to think about it." Rachel nudged his side as he walked past her.

"Why not? If it's alive, it might be friendly."

"Or it might be a group of people who could kill us? I wish it would stop. The noises are what stop me from sleeping. Even when they aren't there, I think I can hear them."

"Okay, Rach. I'm sorry. I didn't mean to make you

feel worse. Only thinking out loud."

"Shush, both of you." I said to them. "We don't know what it is, and we don't know where it is. If you don't keep quiet, it might hear us."

Both nodded at me, silence falling over us. Daniel strode off but made sure Rachel was in grabbing distance in case we stumbled across something. I kept myself at the back, but they followed my pace. Nature hummed around us, ignoring the source of the noises. I took it as a good sign. Wildlife and the continuous hum of the world usually meant there wasn't anything nefarious waiting for us. It was comforting, peaceful. Something I always listened out for. When the world goes still, that's when you want to worry, right?

More time passed. The sound of something following us had stopped. I can't say for sure how long it was. I don't know if it was minutes, hours, seconds, or what, but we felt safe. Surely that's what counts? Although everything seemed okay, it made me worried as well. What if whatever was following us had also slowed down? That either meant zombies had managed to develop reasoning skills, or we weren't being followed by a zombie.

"Can you hear anything?" I whispered, unwilling to disturb the calm wrapping around us.

The twins shook their heads in response. They still seemed on edge. Rachel shifted closer to Daniel. Pulling what little comfort she could from his presence by her side.

"I can't either." I looked around us, "come on. Let's head that way. The trees look like they're packed together. We might be able to find somewhere to hide. If we need to." I took off to my right, hoping the other two would follow close behind.

I tried to hide my worry. To stop it scrawling across my face for Rachel and Daniel to see. Any extra minutes of peace I could give them, would be enough. Would my plan to take cover let the mask slip? I couldn't help it, I felt too exposed. Too out in the open. I half glared at the bright blue sky. I felt like it was mocking us. All those years of awful weather and now, when low visibility would have been perfect, we were flooded with light.

My heart slowed as we drifted under the canopy of trees. The density gave better cover than where we had been walking.

"As long as we don't follow any of the well-worn paths, we should be able to keep hidden." I spoke.

"Do we have enough food to be under here?" Daniel asked.

"I'm not sure." I admitted. "But this is only to make sure whatever was following us, loses us. We should be able to get out of here further down."

He nodded back at me.

"We might be able to find some blackberries around here." Rachel said. "I can't remember if they grow in shaded areas, or if they need more sunlight."

"If we're lucky, we'll find something to keep us going. Before anyone goes scouting, we should get some rest. If we find something to crawl under or behind, we might be able to stay hidden in case whoever, or whatever, was tracking us comes this way."

"Hide and wait in the shadows you mean?" Daniel asked.

I shrugged. "We'll know if we were right to be

worried."

"Wait, if we hang around in here too long it might be too dark for us to move on later. Won't that make it easier for a zombie to get us?" Rachel asked.

"I'm hoping not. But we won't be taking a proper rest break. Only a short one to check we aren't being followed and to get out of their path."

"So, we won't be travelling in pitch black?" Her eyes turned hopefully toward me.

"I didn't say that."

"Great, a nice dark walk in a creepy looking wood."

"Hasn't it always been on your bucket list?" Daniel teased her.

"C'mon, let's find somewhere quick."

As we looked for somewhere to hide, Daniel fell into step with me. I looked over at him, but he was staring ahead.

"You okay?"

"Yeah, I, sorry." He smiled sheepishly, "lost in my thoughts."

"Need to talk?"

"No, I'm good." He paused but looked like he wanted to ask something else. "Anna, have you always been this outdoorsy?"

The use of my name jarred me. "No." I cleared my throat. "I mean, I liked going outside and going on a walk but not like this. I'd never slept outside before. I think I maybe sat in a tent once. It wasn't my sort of thing."

"You could have fooled me." He smiled at me. "Thanks, for trying to keep us safe."

The tension left my shoulders. "Any time."

I've made sure Rachel and Daniel have safely hidden away. We might have to hide between a bush and the base of a tree, no don't ask me what type, but it will keep us out of view. Having other people to look out for has given me more of a reason to be here. More of a reason to survive. It's bittersweet, I would give anything for this to be my own family that I was looking out for. I hope they're safe out there. I hope they've managed to find it to safety.

Days 27, 28, and 29

We never heard anything following us after we entered the trees a few days ago. I don't know if that's a good thing or not. It could mean that we'd been imagining the noises, or whoever or whatever it was had decided to find a different way to track us. There I go with my doom spiralling. Even without anything coming across our paths, we stuck to the trees for the rest of that day. We angled ourselves in the general direction we'd been going before. Eventually, we spilt out into the quiet of the night.

"Rach, Anna, does that look like a building to you?" Daniel asked pointing towards more darkness.

I squinted. My eyes struggling to see anything more than a few feet in front of me. "Not sure. I can only see black."

"There's a shadow line." He outlined with his hand, but I still couldn't make it out. "One sec, I'll take a look and see."

"Don't go." Rachel said as he took off in the direction he'd been looking.

I closed the distance between us, reassuringly squeezing her arm. "He'll be fine. It doesn't look like it's too far off. We might as well follow as we'll be going roughly that way anyway."

"Okay." She pulled my arm into hers, linking us together. "But you are not going to be able to leave me on my own."

I chuckled. "Don't worry, I don't plan on making any crazy journeys in this darkness."

Despite my assurances, she clung to my arm. Even when Daniel came back towards us a few minutes later, she didn't let up.

"What did you find?"

"I'll show you." He said pulling Rachel from my arm.

I struggled to keep up with them. My steps faltering as I tried to keep an eye out for any obstacles jumping out at me. A few steps behind them, I jolted to a stop. An old farmhouse blocking the way. The windows were cracked, but not broken. The front door sat snugly in its frame.

"Did you go inside?" I asked in wonder. My body moving a few steps forward.

"No, I wanted to come and grab you two. What do you think?"

I took the remaining few steps to reach the building. My fingers skimming the rough, exposed bricks. "I'm thinking if there are enough blankets, we might be able to rest in here a lot longer than we have been doing."

I turned to face them. Daniel smiled at me. Rachel

looked at me and I could see the relief washing over her. We might have had to walk through the darkest parts of the night before, but I knew that she'd never really enjoyed it. I moved towards the front door, hoping that it wasn't so snug because it was stuck in its frame.

"3...2...1.." I pulled with more force than I needed. I staggered back as the heavy, oak door swung towards me. I peered into the darkness spilling from the house. "Hello?" I called out, not expecting a response.

After a few moments, I beckoned for the twins to follow me. I took a few steps into the building, enjoying the warmth four walls can bring.

"You two check what the rooms are like and if there's anywhere that we can get a good night's sleep. I'll check the kitchen."

"Sure." Rachel said as their footsteps drifted from me.

I opened all the cupboards but there wasn't anything worth salvaging. A few packets of rotten biscuits, and half a loaf of mouldy bread. If we couldn't find any food here, we'd have to cut the stay short. I stood in the middle of the kitchen. I spiralled slowly, forcing my eyes to look in every corner of the room. I almost gave up when I noticed a small door in the wall.

"Please have something good in here." I whispered to myself.

Pulling the small door free, I was greeted with a few rows of tins. I can't remember the last time I'd been this lucky. I pulled the tins from their shelves and stacked them on the wooden table. There was the usual selection of things: carrots; sweetcorn; peas; and tinned fish. They might not have been the best choices, but they would keep us going for a few days.

The sound of footsteps pulled me from my thoughts and my task of separating the food into three.

"Anna?" Rachel asked as she walked into the kitchen.

"Yeah."

"There's a couple of beds in here, and they're still made up. D'you, mind if me and Daniel take a nap?"

"Go ahead. I'll stay up for a little longer and wake you if I hear anything."

"You're the best." She said, darting forward for a brief hug before heading back to one of the bedrooms.

My mind was too wired to sleep. I wouldn't let them suffer if it would make them feel better in the long run. Intending to find something fresh to change into, I headed in the direction I'd seen Anna go. There were bedrooms at the back of the house. One had been taken over by the twins. In less than 10 minutes they had managed to drop off. I envied them. Leaving them to their rest, I entered the next room.

There were a couple of dressers in the corner by the bed. I drifted closer to one. Looking for something that would fit, but would also not be too easily spotted. The hot pink top I picked up first was quickly discarded. I rummaged through a few drawers before I found a few t-shirts that were black or grey. These would keep me going for a few more months. I tried to place the discarded clothes back where I'd found them. But the need to sleep descended on me.

Day 30

I awoke to the light drifting through the curtain. Startled, I pulled myself from the bed, upending myself on the floor. The thud must have been louder than I thought as I heard two sets of feet rushing towards me.

"Anna? Where are you? Are you alright?" Rachel frantically asked, throwing things around the room.

"I'm okay, I'm okay." I said, slowly rising from my place on the floor. "I forgot where I was for a second. I didn't realise a cosy bed would set off such a panic though."

"I thought a zombie or something had got in with you." Rachel tittered.

"Nope, just this bed right here." I patted it while grinning at them.

"As long as it was nothing serious." Daniel rolled his eyes at us before walking out of the room.

"What's his problem?" I asked Rachel as I straightened out my clothes.

"Oh, he's always been like that. Always sullen.

Don't take it personally."

"I'll try not to. Did you see the food in the kitchen?"

"The small pyramids you made?" Rachel asked as we walked towards the centre of the house.

"Yeah."

"We saw them. I hope you don't mind we took two of them and packed them up already."

"That was the plan. I was going to find you some spare clothes to take, or at least something to help keep you warm when the temperature drops. But I couldn't see a lot. I grabbed a couple of t-shirts for me."

"You don't need to look out for us like this." She said, smiling at me.

"I know, but I might as well. It freed up some time for you today."

"Don't worry about the clothes, I'll grab Danny and we can rummage through them now."

She peeled off towards the living room as I continued to the kitchen. I scooped the remaining pile of tins and placed them in my bag. I felt restless. In the past couple of months, I'd not had the chance to stop and take a second to decompress. To think about the world around me. In this house, I felt safe. The safest I'd felt in a long time. There were no signs that the apocalypse had reached this place. Could we make this our own haven? A place to build. I couldn't let the hope settle in too heavily in my mind. There was no way to keep this building secure.

Day 30 cont.

"Anna, wake up, wake up, wake up, wake up!"

Rachel shook me as she repeated her mantra. My mind responded slowly from the intrusion of my slumber. Grogginess clouded my thoughts as I tried to force myself to wake. She shook me again. My eyes focused on her face, finally noticing the agitation in her movements.

"I'm up. What's wrong?" I stifled a yawn.

"I've seen one of them." She said in a quiet voice.

"One of them what?"

"A zombie. I saw it through the kitchen window."

I scrambled from the bed, pulling my rucksack over my shoulder as I picked it up. I grabbed the cricket bat from beside the door as I tiptoed from the room.

"Does Daniel know?"

She shook her head. Fear stopping her voice.

"Go on, go wake him up and don't forget your bags. We need to find a way to get out of here before it spots us."

"Okay." She squeaked as she raced to where Daniel rested.

I squeezed the handle of the cricket bat as I made sure my bag was securely fastened to me. If I made it through this, I didn't want to end up with no food. I edged closer to the kitchen, listening for any sign that it was in the house with us.

"We need to be careful with this." I said as they entered the kitchen behind me. "Where did you say you saw it, Rachel?"

"It was on the front bit over there." She pointed out of the window in front of us.

"Did you see what direction it was going? Was that the only one you saw?"

"I only saw that one. I don't know if there are any others. I ran straight to you, to wake you up. It didn't look like it knew where we were. It was more meandering its way to the house. Not in a straight path, but it was getting closer."

"Okay. I'll have a look and see if it's still there. Get down. Both of you. I don't know if it will be able to track us inside the house. If I can help it, I'd rather keep you two safe and out of the way."

Both ducked behind the table as I moved to the window. I peered through the pane. My heart pounding through my head. I couldn't see anything. I lowered the bat, resting it against my leg. Maybe it had moved away when Rachel had woken me. As the small seed of hope began to move through me, I heard shuffling from outside. I pushed my face further into the window, but I still couldn't see anything. I couldn't be certain the noise I heard was that, but I couldn't think of any type of animal that would be able to make the same sort of shuffling sound.

"We need to find a way to get out of here that isn't through this room. I don't think we'd be able to get past anything if it is out there."

I moved slowly back towards the table. Slower, and quieter than I had before.

"Have either of you seen a way that we can get out of here?" I risked a quick look before me.

Rachel shook her head, but Daniel looked up.

"I'm sure I saw somewhere yesterday. I thought it would be a good place to try and get out of here in a hurry." He slunk his bag over his back as he stood up. "Come on Rach, we'll survive this together."

He grabbed her hand pulling her to one of the back rooms in the house. I followed quickly behind them, anxious that any loud noises might alert the thing outside to where we were. I tried to brush off Daniel's comment about surviving this with Rachel. I know they're family, but I thought we would all want each other to get out of this alive. I thought over the past couple of weeks that I might be more important to them than that.

"How can we leave?" Rachel asked. "There's no door."

"With this window." He said pointing out his escape plan. "It's lower than any of the others and look where it leads."

I drifted to the window and looked outside. At first, I didn't realise what I was looking at. Then it hit me. The trees backed up to the house. There was an open space between us and the line of trees, but it should be close enough to reach. If we could get out of the window.

"This looks perfect." I turned to them. "Make sure those bags are secure on you. If we lose any of us, at least we will have some food to survive until we can find each other again."

Rachel pulled her straps tighter and tied the ends together in a knot around her waist. Daniel only checked to see if both straps were over his shoulders.

The window was a little way off the floor, not something you could have climbed out of easily. I looked around and saw a chair in the corner of the room. The only issue I had was the floor beneath the window was wooden. I quickly ran to the bathroom and grabbed some of the towels from the cupboard, placing them beneath the opening. There was a light thud as the chair was gently placed on top. I waited, holding my breath. When I was sure it hadn't been heard, I turned to the window.

The window was one of those old, sliding ones. The ones that would fall ceiling to floor if they weren't propped open. I cast my eyes around the room, looking for something to keep it open.

"Have you seen the stick for this?" I whispered to Daniel.

"No, I didn't know it needed one."

"We could use the cricket bat, but I don't want to have to leave it here. We need to find where it is."

He nodded before moving to look around the room. Rachel moved to the other side doing what she could. I stayed by the window. My eyes never leaving the view of the trees. If we could keep this path safe, we could be free.

"I think I've found it." Rachel said as she held up a piece of wood.

I squinted. "It looks about right. Pass it over."

She took a few steps forward before stretching her arm out, offering the pole. I gingerly slid the window up. I wedged the wood in as far to the side as I could get it.

"There should be enough room for us to get out without knocking it. Who wants to run for their lives first?"

"I will," Daniel said stepping towards me. "If the coast is clear, Rachel can follow me."

"I'll make sure the chair doesn't move too much. And remember, don't make any crazy loud noises." I rested the cricket bat against the wall so I could grab the chair with both hands.

Daniel slowly made his way over to me. He nodded his head as he climbed on the chair before darting through the window. He landed with a soft thud on the grass outside. His first few steps in the open were slow. When he felt safe, he quickened his pace. He reached the trees and turned around, signalling for Rachel to follow him. I helped her quickly climb the chair and scramble through the window. She didn't take any time to run towards her brother. As soon as she reached his side, she turned to check it was okay for me to follow.

I took a slow, steadying breath as I perched on the chair. I hooked one leg through the open window. Bracing myself, I launched through the opening into an ungraceful fall onto the grass below. I landed with a thud on my side and heard the chair crash to the floor.

"Anna!" Rachel shouted at me.

I look up and saw the last thing I wanted. A zombie starting to round the corner of the building.

"Oh shit."

I scrambled to my feet, putting distance between me and the creature in front of me. I was hoping this one wouldn't be able to see us. Or hear us. It couldn't be a trait of all of them, but maybe I could get lucky this once.

"It's okay Anna. You can do this." I whispered to myself, looking to see if there was anything I could distract it with. I looked up towards the tree line to see if Rachel and Daniel were safe. They'd disappeared. I couldn't blame them. I wouldn't want to stick around to be dessert either.

I instinctively went to grab the bat from my bag. My fingers grasped empty air. My stomach dropping as I remember placing it by the window. I needed to get it back. My eyes flickered to the approaching zombie. Did I have time to go back? Without it, I didn't give myself much of a chance. I changed direction as I slowly moved back towards the window. Daniel was right. It wasn't too far from the ground. But I'd need to turn my back on the zombie to grab it. I paced with my hand outstretched behind me. My heart beating faster, the feeling turning my stomach. Now didn't feel like the best time to be sick.

After what felt like an eternity but had maybe been ten seconds, my hand bumped into the outer edge of the house. I risked a quick look behind me. I thanked whatever had decided to watch over me. I was within arm's distance of the window. I quickly checked on the zombie. It had barely made any headway in coming towards me. Maybe it didn't know I was here? I took a deep breath and quickly moved to my right and turned to reach into the building. I knew the bat was underneath the window. I hoped I hadn't knocked it over when I capsized the chair.

As I ran my hands over the wall, edging closer to the window, I took a quick look back towards the zombie. It had stopped. Frozen, seemingly to be doing nothing. It made me more anxious than I'd been before.

I pushed myself onto my tiptoes. With the extra reach, I managed to grasp the handle. I snatched the bat through the window and quickly turned around. It was still standing there, but now it looked like it was staring straight at me. I hugged the bat to me, fighting the urge to run as fast as I could. I started to move back towards where I'd edged myself before. Struggling to keep my flight mode under control. I needed to keep as much distance between us as possible. I'd like to think if it came to a race, I'd be able to outrun the undead, but I didn't want to get too cocky and optimistic.

I'd not taken my eyes off that thing since I grabbed the bat, and it still hadn't moved anywhere. I knew my only chance of survival would be if I could get to the tree line before it. Or, and it was a big or, I could try to kill it. The second option didn't leave me with a lot of hope, not given my past encounters with them. I took a few more steps to my left, angling towards the trees. It was weird to think this could be the end of my life. I felt like I was literally staring death in the face with no relief from anywhere.

It was when I'd almost given up, I heard a noise to my right. Sounding out from inside the house. I couldn't make out what it was, but it sounded like things being thrown around and toppled over. It wasn't until I heard a voice, I realised what had happened.

"Over here, you dead monster. Look at us!"

Rachel and Daniel had circled and gone back inside. I felt grateful to them but also annoyed they'd risked themselves to help me. I couldn't argue with the results though. It was working. The zombie no longer stared at me but moved towards the window. I didn't know how those two would make it out of there. So, I did something I never thought I'd do. Something no one would have thought I'd do. I ran at the thing with my bat raised.

I don't know if I'm an idiot or what, but I managed to surprise the zombie before I thwacked it over the head. I know I wasn't able to hit the last one as hard as I did this, and even then, I didn't kill it in one hit. I had angered it. I had made it realise I was there. I took a couple of steps back before I raised the cricket bat to hit it again. As the wooden bat landed on its head, the crack of the skull fracturing reached my ears. I exercised every bit of control I had over myself to stop myself from throwing up.

I continued to hit it. With every successful contact, it slowed. I don't know how long it took. I don't know how long I was hitting it when it had stopped. Eventually, I slowed my movements. My mind catching up with the scene in front of me. I'd managed to bludgeon to death my first zombie. It didn't make me feel good. The sight of the body on the ground next to me, and the blood and brains covering my bat made me throw up. I couldn't hold it back any longer. I was thankful when Rachel and Daniel came running up to me with some cloths. I used one to clean my face and another to wipe down the bat. I didn't want all that drying on it when I was carrying it with me. The thought itself made me heave, but luckily nothing else came up.

"Shall we go?" I asked them through deep breaths.

They nodded in response, and we headed towards the trees. My thoughts hoping we would be able to find safety at some point.

Day 31

We're hiding. As if yesterday's event wasn't bad enough already, we've now come across something we've never encountered before. Not together, or separately. I can barely see the page well enough to write this down. It doesn't matter though. We might not be able to see what's out there, but we can hear it. We can hear every laboured breath it takes. I'm worried the scratching of my pen will draw it to us, but I can't let this go. I can't let this night pass without keeping a clear record.

I'm hoping it can't hear us. That it can't hear our breaths. The short, sharp intakes we're trying hard not to take. I feel like we're breathing too loudly. Most of the day we've run. Someone has found us. Well, I'm assuming it's a person as I've never seen a zombie behave like this before. It sounded so angry and aggressive. Not the usual snarls and growls which accompany their rotting forms. Whatever this thing is. It's freaked all three of us out.

Rachel and Daniel are sleeping. Terror and exhaustion are not a good combination. This small respite of sleep might help clear their minds. It might be the thin line between life and death. I don't mind going without for a little if it saves them. They both settled and drifted off, but I can still hear it.

There were some houses nearby, but we didn't want to be easily found. Would it know to look for us in a house? I didn't want to risk it and pushed us into a hedgerow. I guess that's one of the good things about travelling near minimal woodland. There's always a space to hide if you get desperate. I'd pushed Rachel and Daniel into one section before moving further down from them. I didn't want my being awake to draw anything to them. It was a risk I wasn't willing to take. My hiding spot was more painful to wriggle into, but the cuts and scrapes were more than worth it.

I've looked out a few times. Peering through the criss-cross of nature. Nothing is out of place, at least from my limited knowledge of what is normal. After yesterday, I'd been feeling braver. I wasn't as defenceless as I'd been telling myself. It wasn't all luck and cowardice keeping me alive. With my trusty cricket bat by my side, I'd ventured out into the clearing.

Thinking back on it, I feel foolish. What if I'd been caught? I'd stopped every few seconds to listen. The wind whispered around me, rustling the leaves underfoot. Other than that, I was wrapped in calm. An easy stillness had fallen around us. I let myself breathe normally. Whoever or whatever had followed us was nowhere to be seen. Maybe they'd become bored and wandered off when they couldn't find us anymore? A stupid part of me wanted to search it out, stop it from causing any more pain. The risk I had been avoiding since this started tried to seduce me. I edged forward, a few short, tentative steps away from safety. I couldn't leave Rachel and Daniel. My movements faltered. I couldn't abandon them while they slept. Not after they risked themselves for me. We were safe. No need to tempt fate anymore.

Day 32

The world has changed. There isn't the feeling of being followed or watched that we had yesterday. Maybe today will be a normal day? As dawn broke over us, I woke Rachel and Daniel and we set out. Calm drifted over us, causing our stumbled steps to falter with shock at the scene we were greeted with.

How do I describe it? Are there words that can be used to explain the jolt that ricocheted through me? One second we were skirting around the edge of Beacon Hill and the next we stumbled across a battleground. Warning signs may have been scattered around us as we walked, but I'd missed them all. If we hadn't, we might have saved ourselves this small feeling of horror.

"Did you see that?" Rachel asked, peering towards the grass.

"See what?" Daniel asked her.

She shook her head. "Never mind, I must have imagined it."

I turned to look at the spot she'd been gazing at. Nothing stood out to me.

"Wait." Daniel said.

I halted my steps, looking around us when I saw it. What I had mistaken for puddles of water looked deeper, looked darker. My heart faltered beneath my breast as I tried to convince myself I was wrong. I took a couple of anxious steps forward and looked at the puddle. The water was almost black. I threw a twig towards it. Instead of the smooth splash of a puddle, my grim reality was confirmed. Blood.

"Eurgh, that's disgusting." Daniel said, holding his hand over his mouth. "I think I'm going to throw up."

I followed his gaze. The scattered humanoid remains separating themselves from the shadows the more I stared. The pieces were strewn all around us. Something terrible had happened here. From the limbs and scattered body parts, it made me think some giant monster had ripped the unsuspecting people limb from limb. I'd never seen anything like it before. I didn't want to again.

The wind picked up and swirled the stench of death and decay around us, replacing the usual hints of damp soil and bark. It felt as though it had been waiting for us to see the carnage before allowing the smell to hit us. Using it to the best effect.

Daniel's face paled as he tried to keep the contents of his stomach in his body.

"Do you want to move? Get away from here?" I asked him, taking a step closer.

He withdrew from me but nodded sharply. "I didn't think we'd try and make camp here." He said weakly.

"No, although it might keep anything else away from us."

"Will it be safe to go back where we came?" Rachel squeaked out.

"At least for a little bit." I looked at them both, not sure who was more at risk of losing their breakfast. "Will you be able to get out of here?"

"I hope so."

"Yes."

They answered at the same time.

Rachel moved over to her brother and grabbed him by the arm. I turned and made my way back the way we came. Moving slowly so the twins didn't have to rush behind me.

"I wonder what happened back there." Daniel said, his voice returning to its usual cadence.

"A massacre."

"But why?" He mused.

"I don't want to know. If I don't think about it, I might be able to get out of here okay." Rachel said.

Daniel ignored her. "What do you reckon Anna? Any thoughts on what might have happened?"

"Honestly? I'm not sure. A massacre for sure, but I don't know why. It seems calculated. Nothing I've seen from the zombies. They wouldn't waste that much person, and I've never seen them pull someone apart like that. It's always been cleaner, if biting into someone can count as clean. It seemed so fresh, it can't have happened more than a few hours ago." I paused, allowing the nausea to fade. "I think I'm with Rachel, dwelling on this is making my stomach turn."

Daniel didn't say anything else as he took in the scenery behind us. His face paled the longer he looked at it. I don't think he could stop himself. His hand covered his sister's which was wrapped around his arm. I couldn't tell if that was for his comfort or hers. At that moment, I don't think it mattered.

The macabre scene behind us set me on edge. I didn't like that I couldn't figure it out. How long ago had it happened? Was it what had been following us? Was it a coincidence? Would we need to run before what had caused it came back? The only piece of hope I had, that I could let my mind pass over, was that it was a person, or a group of people who had done this. That someone was hunting zombies, and this was the result. As much as that thought filled me with hope, it also filled me with dread. If there was someone out there that could do that, we wouldn't want to run into them. This could be our ending.

"C'mon, if we go round here, we might be able to bypass that site but get some distance in. Hopefully, the smell puts off any of the undead that might want to feast on us."

I didn't wait for a response as I began to skirt around the edge of the scene. I kept as much distance between us and the destruction as I could. My eyes searching for any signs that this had dragged out further than we anticipated. Some slight signs of disturbance waved through the undergrowth, but we were spared the worst of it. I didn't want to think about what had happened, but I couldn't stop myself. I imagined a group of people who all turned into zombies and attacked each other. I shivered at the thought.

Day 32 cont.

A few hours have passed since we stumbled across the bodies. Although we were no longer haunted by the decay and debris that had scattered around the area, it wasn't far from our minds. I had been fighting with the images and thoughts that had been filtering through my mind since. What if we were never able to stop this virus, or disease, or whatever it was? Had anyone worked out what had caused this yet? It might not be as quick as a change as we thought. I don't know how long it took for the first person to become infected and turn. I'd never seen it happen.

There had to be someone out there who could figure out how this had started. Figure out how to save us before we all ended up like the bodies in the woods. Had it spread beyond the UK yet? My thoughts were spiralling until Rachel distracted me.

"D'you think we'll run into whoever did all of that?"

"I really, really hope not. I'm hoping they'll have

gone in a different direction. One where they can cause more death and destruction far away from where we'll be."

"What do you think happened? I can't stop thinking about it. No matter how hard I try and think of something else. My mind wanders back to those pools of blood." Daniel said. His voice low, emotion bubbling across his words. "I've never seen so much blood in one place."

"It's alright." I said reaching across to him. "We should be okay as long as we keep moving and stay out of the way."

"That's what you believe?" He asked, his eyes flashing to my face. "You think we can be safe if we keep moving?"

"No, I don't think any of us are safe." I tried to keep my voice calm. "How can we be safe when we are in the middle of a zombie apocalypse? But if we stay in one place, and too close to what we've gone past I think we'll be sitting ducks. I don't know what caused it. Two groups of people, some people hunting zombies, a group of people who turned at the same time. I don't have the answers. I can't explain it. But we can be optimistic that we can stay ahead of what caused it. That we won't suffer from the same fate."

Shock from my honesty rested on his face. "Thanks," he mumbled. "I guess you're right. We can't sit around waiting for something to come and attack us."

"You think it might be a group of people who did that?" Rachel asked, disgust dripping from her voice.

"It could be, but I don't know how. If it was, I don't think we want to meet them. They don't seem to be a friendly bunch."

"I don't know," Daniel said. "It might be useful to meet them. They could keep us safe. Let us tag along with them while they look for their next target."

"How would we know their next target wasn't us? They might offer to help us then use us as bait for their next hunt. I'd rather stay away."

"I'm with Anna, Danny. I don't think those are people who would want to look out for us. What would we have to offer in return?"

"Hey, it was only a thought. I didn't say we should go out of our way to find them." He held his hands up.

We carried on slowly through the area. Cautious of where we stood. Checking the ground to make sure it was clear of anyone. I don't know if I could manage stumbling across something like that again. I didn't think I could be surprised by anything else, then something like this happens. I could feel my calmness fraying, but I wouldn't let it go. Not when others depended on me.

We travelled further in one go than we had for the past few days. The horror haunting us and pushing us further from that spot. The idea of settling down anywhere near it made my skin crawl. And as much as he might not want to show it, I think it would affect Daniel as badly as it had Rachel and me. He tried not to let people in, but that didn't mean it was any easier on him.

Daniel volunteered to take the first watch. Maybe it had bothered him more than he let on? Usually, he jumped at the chance to rest and zone out, but he seemed more on edge. I don't know what was racing through his mind, and I didn't ask. If he wanted to talk to us about it, he wouldn't be keeping it to himself.

Rachel was more open, her thoughts and feelings showed whether she wanted them to or not. Her fears tumbled from her mouth, rushing to escape, and let her inner mind feel free for a brief moment. She seemed comfortable around me. It was nice. I felt like family, maybe not paternal, there isn't anybody who would think that. I felt more like a responsible aunt, distant but close. Someone you could look up to, but also get into trouble with. If only I felt as mature as I saw my aunts.

Day 33

Even with the dreaded scene left behind us, I still felt on edge. No matter what I did to shake the feeling, I worried. When would we next stumble across something like that? Would we find ourselves in the path of what had caused it? How would I keep us safe? If there were only one or two people, we could make it out okay. But if there were a group of them? I didn't like our odds. The more I dwelled on it, the more I thought it had to be a group to have caused the mess.

On the plus side, there was a group of people going around the countryside hunting and killing zombies. On the downside, there was a group of people going around the countryside hunting and killing. There's no way we would be able to tell if the people who were part of what we'd seen were only killing zombies. Could people revert to their base animal instinct? Once they got a taste of killing, would it be the only thought that crossed their mind?

If only trust was something you could have for the

people you run into. Not everyone would be willing to help. If I hadn't been so lonely, would I have helped Daniel and Rachel? Maybe not. If it wasn't for me, they might still be struggling to get the supplies they needed. I like to think I've given them a survival plan, but I bet not everyone would have reacted in the same way. I mean, who would have done? They tried to steal from me. I gave them a chance. Does that mean I should give everyone the same chance?

"Anna?" Rachel asked, "d'you know where we're going? We don't seem to have moved out of these trees for a while."

I paused, looking at the nature surrounding us. "Er, I have a rough idea. I might've gotten us twisted round. I don't know where we should be going, and I'm hoping the route we're on will keep us safe. Or at least safer than we have been."

"That's not exactly filling me with hope." She tittered. "I was hoping you would have a better sense of direction than me. Sticking to safe sounds like a good option as well. D'you think we'll bump into anyone out here?"

"We could. After what we saw yesterday, and whatever was following us, I'd say there's a good chance. We can hope they've moved on, or at least hope that if we bump into anything, it's friendly, and doesn't want to kill us on sight."

"Thanks, Anna, I feel 100% better already."

"It's what I'm here for." I chuckled darkly. "Stop." I continued, "we're going to have to make a choice. It looks like we can follow one trail out of the woods, or we can head deeper in."

"Which d'you reckon's safer?" Rachel asked.

"Not a clue. Either could lead to safety or both could lead to death. I don't know how severely affected this area of the country is."

"If we head out of the trees, we might be able to stumble across more houses for food. But if we head further in, we might be able to forage a little better. How much food did we get from the cottage?" Daniel asked.

"Not sure, maybe enough for a week at least. It could have been a little longer. I know there were some leftover tins, I packed a couple of them. Not sure about you two? One option would be to ration out the food even more. Not the best plan, but it would give us a few more days."

"So, we'd need to find more to eat."

It wasn't a question, but I answered him anyway. "More than likely, unless it doesn't take us long to get through here and stumble across a farm or something. I'm not sure whereabouts we are, so I don't know if we'll be able to find much either way. But we should all decide where we go. Either could be the wrong choice and I don't want any one person blamed. Which do you think's best?"

"Hmm," Daniel mulled over his words. "I vote for going further in. The zombies don't look like they are heading this far into the trees, and we might be able to keep relatively safe. What do you think, Rach?"

"I'd like to be out of the creepy woods. I feel like anything could be lurking and waiting for us."

"Did you notice any zombies hiding behind trees when it was just us?"

"I hate it when you're right. But no. We travelled easier when we were covered in the more forest-like areas. Something puts them off venturing in them. I still want to be in the open. Find a nice, dry place to sleep with walls and a roof." Rachel looked over her shoulder, towards the darker part of the woods. "But I also don't want to get trapped in a house or something. Just waiting for them things to come and get us. I think I'd prefer the bugs and spiders. Maybe."

"Okay, deep, dark woods it is then. I'm sure we can find somewhere or something to give us a bit of roof when we stop for longer. If that makes you feel better?" I said smiling.

"It might, a little. As long as it doesn't fall on us!"

"That is not part of the deal." I laughed. "I can only offer questionable wooden structures. No safety certificates."

"C'mon you two, we don't want to hang around here too long. Not if we want to make some headway before it gets too dark."

"Okay, Captain Daniel. We'll follow your lead."

He muttered something under his breath as he started to make his way off the path we'd been following.

"Ignore him, he likes to complain but I think he's glad we've got you." Rachel whispered to me as we followed after him.

I knew it had been a group decision, but I didn't really want to go this way. I knew we'd be able to hide better, but the idea of being stuck in the woods freaked me out. Too many horror films in my teens had given me a skewed view of the type of people and creatures you might bump into.

Daniel was a better leader than I'd been. He checked the route we were going and made sure there were no hidden holes or stuck out roots. We followed his path with ease with little changes to the line he made. Even though he was a good half a foot taller than either of us, he'd made sure we could manage it without falling behind. I was thankful, I didn't enjoy having to climb around places. Being outside was enough for me without any gruelling hikes added to the mix.

The further we ventured in, the more the trees began to interlock. The sky overhead became a blanket of red and golden leaves, blocking out any view of the outside world. Daniel slowed his pace as the route before us darkened with the fading light.

"Which way do you want to go?" He shouted over his shoulder. "We could go in a sort of straight line, or we could veer off towards the light. We'd be able to travel for longer, but we could get lost."

"Whichever, I think we might be lost enough as it is."

"Your choice Danny. I'm already in here now, it doesn't matter what happens."

"Okay, keep close. Let's see if we can get some light back."

We didn't walk for much longer before Daniel stopped us again. The diagonal path we'd taken hadn't given us as much light as he'd hoped for.

"Let's make a roof for Rachel. There's enough light to be able to put a quick lean-to together."

"Do you know how to make a lean-to?" I asked.

He stared at me. "You've never made a den before?"

"Do I look like the sort of person to make dens?"

He looked me up and down for a second. "No. I

guess you don't." He turned to Rachel. "Can you grab some of those longer branches and drag them back here?"

"I can try, but if I touch an insect, I won't be able to stop the scream."

"We'll wait for it." He rolled his eyes. "Anna, can you help me pull these around these trees?"

"Sure." I dropped my bag near where he'd pointed and began moving the branches and twigs around.

I looked at the thick branches littering the floor, and the thinner pieces Rachel dragged over to us. It wouldn't be the same as a house, but it would give us some comfort for the night. It would keep the wind off us at least.

"Daniel, can you help me wedge this one here?" I asked as I tried to lift the heavy branch.

It took longer than anticipated, but we were able to put something together. Lean-to was a good descriptor for the haphazard structure we'd built. Now, as long as it stayed upright and didn't collapse on us while we slept. It seemed sturdy enough, but I didn't want to touch it too much. There was no need to tempt whatever deity or omniscient presence which might be watching us.

"Okay, who's going on first watch?"

"I will," Daniel said. "I don't feel much like resting, apart from stretching out my legs."

"Okay. If I doze off, wake me up and I'll take the next one."

Day 34

Daniel shook my shoulder.

"Anna, wake up."

"Wh-what is it?"

"There's someone out there."

I rubbed the sleep from my eyes. "You sure?"

"I don't know. I can't see anything, but I heard something."

"Okay, wake Rachel. We might need to run."

He nodded before moving around me to wake his sister. If I could sleep with walls around me and not be woken up by either twin, it would be a price too high to pay. I strained my ears to listen out for what had caused Daniel to disturb us. The creaks and moans of the trees reverberated around us. If there was anyone out there, they were masked. I risked a glance to check Rachel was awake and they both had their bags with them. Even though I hadn't heard anything, I didn't want to risk it. It was safer to be cautious. I'd rather be cautious and alive, than adventurous and dead.

We stayed still, trying to minimise any noise we might make. Time rolled agonisingly slow as though we were pushing a heavy rock up a hill. I attempted to count the seconds. To give some order to our struggle. Nothing. No sounds, no noises that popped out at us. I was starting to question if Daniel had heard anything until I noticed something.

The noise was faint, really faint. It was the almost unmistakable sound of talking. It sounded far off, but it was still people. The words were too low and garbled for me to understand, but I could hear them. I looked at Daniel and Rachel, to see if they were making a noise. When I caught their eyes, they both shook their heads slightly. I didn't know how to respond. From the sound of it, the people were some distance from us. It didn't stop the pounding of my heart. They could have been the ones responsible for the massacre. They could quite easily make our little camp into the same sort of scene.

Adrenaline coursed through me. Fight or flight. Stay or run. I squeezed the handle of the cricket bat. It would be easy enough to run. If we knew where we could run to. I took control of my thoughts. No, the best plan would be to stay put until we could figure out where to go. Panic simmered under the calm I forced on myself.

"Where do you think they are?" Daniel whispered.

"I don't know. Not close, or at least far enough away." I whispered back.

"Do you think we could hide the shelter a little? Make sure they don't know what it is they're looking at?"

"I scattered leaves over it and tried to blend it in

with all the other fallen branches. As long as they don't realise there's an opening, we should be fine."

He started to pull away from Rachel.

"What are you doing?" I hissed at him.

"Covering the entrance." He almost seemed to shrug as he sidled past me.

"Daniel—" Rachel whispered.

"I'll be fine." He said cutting off the rest of her sentence.

I moved closer to her, both of us seeking comfort in the other's presence. He shuffled through the discarded branches we hadn't been able to use. He tested each one, I'm not sure what for before he started piling them up around the slight gap. He wove the bendier pieces together, all the leaves sticking out towards the outside world.

"That should help." He whispered as he moved back towards us.

"I hope it works."

"It's stopped the opening from being seen head-on, but I'm not sure if it will keep us undetected completely."

"And it should stop a bit more of the cold." Rachel said as she pulled her coat around her.

"Good points." I strained to hear any other sounds coming from outside. "Let's try and get a bit more rest before we head out. I'll keep an ear out. If we give it enough time, we should be able to get away without anyone noticing."

Daniel nodded as he fluffed his bag into a makeshift pillow.

"Will you be okay, Anna?" Rachel asked.

"As okay as any of us have been the past few

months. Daniel's handiwork should make it more difficult, and we might blend in a little more now." I smiled at her. "Get some more rest, Rachel. There's no point in staying awake and worrying if you don't need to."

"Okay, but don't leave us. I don't know what we would do without you."

"I promise I won't."

I watched her settle back into the same place as before, using her brother for extra warmth. Her words turning over in my mind. Why would she think I'd run off and leave them on their own? I tried to think of anything I'd done that would make her think I'd abandon them. Nothing came to mind. If there was one thing I could do, it would be to make sure both were safe.

Day 34
continued

I thought we were safe. Why could we never be safe? Whoever had been walking around and talking earlier had disappeared. Or at least the traces of them had disappeared. I was lulled by my own overconfidence we could survive this. I thought they were too far away to spot us. I didn't think they would venture this way. I don't like to admit when I'm wrong, but I was wrong. Maybe I wasn't paying enough attention to the world around me. I don't know how I could have missed it. One second it was quiet. The next I could hear as clearly as if they'd been talking to me.

"What's that?" I heard a male voice ask.

"My guess? Somewhere to sleep, if you're a child." Someone responded.

"D'ya reckon there's anyone still in it?" A third asked.

"Not sure." The person paused. "We've not seen anyone round here. And I can't see any signs that anyone has been around here."

"Apart from the shelter?"

"Apart from the shelter."

"Someone must have put it together. It seems too ordered to be an accident. Too constructed. Look, you can see..." the voice muffled. "It won't last long."

"If you think it's new, we'll have a look."

I froze. Stay or run. Stay or run.

I quickly shuffled towards the twins and nudged them awake. Before they could make a sound, I placed my hands across their mouths. When it looked like they understood, I slowly backed away. I pointed outside the shelter. Daniel seemed to understand me.

The heavy crunch of leaves sounded closer to our shelter. Our safety. I'd heard three voices, but it only sounded like one of them was approaching. It didn't matter how many of them had walked towards us, I couldn't think of a way we could escape without being seen. The only positive would be if they didn't want to do us any harm. I couldn't let my mind stray over thoughts of anything bad happening to Rachel or Daniel.

"Stay here. Don't come out until we've gone, or it's safe." I whispered at them.

"Anna, no." I heard Rachel whisper, but I ignored her.

I scooted to the woven entrance, bag secured on my shoulder and stood up.

"Hi" I said to the surprise of the guy stood at the entrance.

"So, someone was in there." He mumbled, half to himself. "I guess Adrian was right."

He turned to look at me. I wanted to take a step

back, the look he passed over me didn't leave me feeling warm and fuzzy.

"Adrian!" The guy in front of me shouted.

"What?"

"There's a woman here."

"Bring her over then."

The guy turned to me again, eyes roaming across me. "Looks like you'll be coming with us."

I took a step forward. He grabbed my arm, tighter than necessary.

"Where are you taking me?" I asked, trying to keep my voice level.

"Don't worry, it's somewhere safe."

I didn't believe him, but I let myself be pulled along. If I kept going forward, they wouldn't look inside and find Daniel or Rachel. If giving myself up kept them safe, it would be worth it. I focused on that as my heart thudded under my chest. At least I kept them safe.

Day 35

There hasn't been any sign of Rachel and Daniel being brought to camp. Something I'm thankful for. I don't know what they want me for. I've been left alone, but I don't like it. Why would you forcefully bring someone with you and then ignore them? Although being ignored is better than several other options. I was brought into the camp, no searches, no questions and then ignored. This must be how lingering souls feel. Endlessly tied down without understanding what's happening.

The guy who'd found me, or who I purposefully stepped in front of, deposited me in the camp then disappeared. From eavesdropping over the past few hours, I'd learnt his name was Nick. I wasn't able to learn much else, except he left camp a lot. Not that I was bothered by that. An unsettling atmosphere clouded around him. The less time I had to spend in his company, the better.

Despite my loneliness, the camp wasn't empty.

Far from it. This was the most number of living people I'd seen in one place since this started. There were only adults, from what I could tell, but they had banded together. Unease still gripped me at being brought here unceremoniously, and with no say in the matter, but I felt safe. No more looking over my shoulder to see if something was coming after me. No more need to sleep for only of hours at a time. Although, I don't think that will be a habit I will be able to shake for a while now.

True, there were a lot of people here, but I wouldn't say they were surviving. The camp looked temporary. There were no buildings, and everyone else seemed more on edge than me. I couldn't confirm it, but I had a feeling these people were behind the destruction we'd seen a few days earlier. The tents were lined neatly and evenly spaced out. I was in a camp, one that was more militaristic than I'd have liked. As an outsider, I couldn't feel like I could relax.

This morning I was brought a warm bowl of what looked like gruel. I never realised that was a real thing, but the lumpy, grey substance in the bowl was all my mind could think of.

"Thanks." I said to the woman who brought it over.

"What for?" She asked.

"The food." I gestured. "I've not had anything warm in months."

She raised her eyebrow. "Why?"

"I didn't want to attract anything to me. It wasn't a risk I was jumping to take on my own." I answered defensively. I'm sure it's alright being a group this big, but for most people, I bet warm food was off the table.

I thought to myself.

"You're an idiot." She scoffed. "They aren't attracted to heat."

"What if I didn't mean zombies?"

She rolled her eyes. "We've been tracking them. Heat isn't something they're looking for."

"Good to know."

She clicked her tongue at me before walking off. The information felt off. If they couldn't sense heat, how had they been finding everyone? The more I learnt or noticed about these, the more I felt like something was wrong with them. Apart from the undead thing.

That was the last contact I had with anyone today. I've been left to myself again, waiting until the light disappears. I've been thinking of making a run for it. Trying to find my way back to Rachel and Daniel. They would have made it safely out by now. There were no walls, or trenches around the camp, only a ring of torches. Enough that anyone watching would see me go. Would they know I wasn't supposed to leave? I didn't want to risk it. I'm still too much of a coward to risk my life.

Day 36

Another day, and still no movement. The tents and lean-tos may look temporary, but the camp feels permanent. I've been welcomed to get food with them, but I'm still being ignored. I want to ask someone what's happening. Find out who's in charge and demand to be let go. Why do they need stragglers and strays? I've been watching how everyone interacts, but I can't place a leader. Or maybe they don't want me to know.

Rachel and Daniel have been on my mind for the past couple of days. I feel awful for leaving them. I hope they know it was to help them. At least they had their supplies, and enough to last them a few more days. They could head out of the trees and find somewhere safe. I hoped they would be able to find the haven they'd been so keen on finding. They had my cricket bat to keep them safe. I'd slipped the knot from around my bag as I made my decision to save them. It might have been a stupid move for me, but they may need it more. Plus, I didn't want to seem threatening. Although, that could be why I've been dragged here.

It's not too bad, but there's something off. I can't quite place it, but it doesn't feel right with me. It could be the lack of safety, the nonchalance of the world. I don't know, but I didn't want to be here. My thoughts spiralled the more I isolated myself. How had we not stumbled across all these people before? How had it taken a small scavenging group to find us?

Day 36
continued

I tried not to dwell. Negative thoughts would not help anyone, especially not me. Come on Anna, it doesn't matter what the reason is it's weird. No matter what the answer was, they didn't look like they were trying to create a safe space for humans to thrive. Every time I moved somewhere, I felt like a million eyes were following me. As long as I didn't go far, I couldn't see me being too much of a problem.

I'd found myself pushed up against a tree, as far away from the rest of them as I could get without suspicion. There's been more activity today than before. I've been watching it from afar, trying to understand something. It's not been much, more bustling and energy from the rest of my new campmates. I'd missed the sign.

"Here, take this."

My train of thoughts derailed as a man I'd not seen before, thrust what looked like a spear into my hands.

"What do I need this for?"

"I'd take it if you don't want to end up dead."

I hurriedly took the makeshift weapon. He motioned for me to follow, and I clumsily trailed behind.

"What will I need this for? Isn't it safe here?"

"We've spotted another zombie. Every able-bodied person has to help out."

"Wait, what? You think I can help kill these things? With this?" I shuddered at the thought of being that close to one again.

"You've stayed alive this long so far. How else have you managed without killing anything? Didn't you get told what we would be doing here when you came back with Nick?"

"Firstly, by being a coward. Secondly, I didn't willingly come back, I was dragged. Literally. My arm was in a vice grip the entire way back here. I have no clue what's happening. This is the first time anyone's told me anything."

The guy stopped walking and turned on me. I cringed back a step. "He dragged you here? That son of a —" He took a breath. "I've told him about that before, we can't be dragging anyone here expecting them to help. I'm sorry you've been brought here without your say so. But we could use your help. Everyone needs to help us all survive."

"Can't I leave instead? It might be better if I did, I could become a liability with this thing." I said waving around my stick. My hopes rising as I spoke.

"I wish we could, but we lost a lot of people recently and we need everyone we can get. If we can find anyone else in the next day, we might be able to spare you, but I'd appreciate it if you could stick around."

"I don't think I'm a good replacement."

"I'm sorry. I'll see what I can do, but it's not up to me."

He looked almost apologetic before he turned and headed to one of the tents at the centre of the camp. I took that as the end of the conversation. It felt better to know I shouldn't have been dragged here. Not that it stopped me from being here. Now I had to figure out how to fight with a spear and hold one without stabbing myself or anyone.

I scanned for anyone practising with any weapons. No practising was happening, but more people were gathered in one corner. Were there corners in this camp? It's not like there was a perimeter wall. They grouped up in the closest thing to a corner I could see. I slunk towards the back of them. No one noticing my arrival. I couldn't help but feel like the universe was mocking me in some way. Thrust into a group to help keep everyone else safe, when I'd barely managed to keep myself safe.

It didn't look like we would be doing anything today. The group were too relaxed. I sank to the floor, pulling my rucksack between my legs and laying my stick next to me. Now was as good a time as any to get some rest. I'm sure I'd know when something had changed.

Day 37

Energy buzzed around me. Pulling me from my rest. I used the spear to push myself to my feet. Everyone else was already on theirs. I tried to see what had caused the change in feeling when I saw him. Nick. I shrank back, trying to hide my face. My gut felt uneasy about him. I didn't want to test if it was right or not.

"One of them's been spotted toward the edge of the woods. It looks to have freshly turned. We know what that means."

People around me cheered. Nick paced in front of the group. All attention was on him, the group hanging on his every word.

"We're lucky there's only one this time. Not like the group last week. This one should be easy. Remember, stay away from its face. Don't get caught where we might have to put you down as well."

Shock covered me as people around me laughed. As though killing someone was a joke. How were they able to go along with this so nonchalantly? I waited for him to say something else, but that was it. There was nothing left to his speech. He turned his back on us, speaking to someone by his side. I felt dazed. Unwilling to believe what I had heard. How could someone be so callous?

"Everyone." Nick said, pointing in the direction he'd started walking.

The group I'd huddled into began to follow. As we moved, I allowed myself to fall back. I noticed again how organised everyone seemed to be. There was no jostling, no shoving. Only a steady, silent stream of movement. How many times had this been done to reach this level of order? How many people had died for it to be perfected to this level?

Blood rushed through my body, making me light-headed. I didn't know what to expect or what was happening. The only positive thing was that they wouldn't put us all in danger. It couldn't be a trap to kill us all. How was I going to make it out alive? I'd not handled myself too well before. Being a coward had always been my best plan, and it had worked. I had been fine until I tried to save someone else. Would I be in this mess if I hadn't saved Rachel and Daniel?

Our steady march was the only sound I could hear through the trees. All sounds of nature drowned out by the steady thud as each foot hit the ground in unison. What I wouldn't give to hear the gentle rustle of the fallen leaves, the sounds of animals running across the ground. Something that didn't remind me of a funeral march.

Suddenly the pace began to slow. I couldn't tell what had caused it, but I followed the people around me. I was too far back to understand what was happening at the front. My mind flittered to escape. Maybe if they were distracted, I could make a break for it. I would have, but where would I go? We slowed to a complete stop and with it my chance to run stopped as well. I felt awkward. The spear resting awkwardly against my body. Calm oozed from the people in line with me. There was no fear, only anticipation.

"First line forward." Nick said, barely audible from where I was stood.

There was a shuffling from the front. I tried to peer over the heads of the people lined before me. I couldn't see what was happening.

"Second line."

More shuffling and this time I could see the group move into the surrounding trees. It was smooth, clean, well-rehearsed. They knew where they needed to be, unlike me.

"Third line."

"Fourth line."

The number of people between me and the ones at the front slowly dwindled. Four more groups of people moved before there were no one to shield us. My stomach lurched. My legs wobbled. I gripped the spear, using it to keep me upright.

"Ninth line."

The people around me began to move. I started to follow them, trying to keep my head down. No such luck. Nick pulled me from the line. Unease settled through me.

"Not you, newbie. You've got a different role."

He pulled me by my arm, dragging me forwards. I struggled to move my legs to match his pace. He shoved me to the floor and pulled a knife from this belt. I scrambled across the floor, fear consuming me.

Nick laughed. "You're not fast enough, sweetheart."

He lunged at me, grabbing my arm once again. I tried to pull free, but I couldn't shake his grip. Before I could register the pain, he sliced through my upper arm.

I shrieked. A dull ache spread through my arm from the point the knife had sliced its way through my skin. It was the warm sensation of blood, however, that made my stomach flip. I grabbed my arm trying, and failing, to squish the wound together. I knew it wouldn't work, but I didn't know what else to do. The pounding in my arm made its way to my head. I couldn't think straight. I felt dizzy. My vision blurred. I blinked rapidly, trying to refocus on the world around me. Once the world stopped spinning, and my breath had calmed, I looked for Nick. He'd disappeared. I tried to turn, but the sensation made me double over. That bastard.

I picked up the spear in my left hand, the weight felt clumsy, but I needed it to stay upright. I didn't know how long I'd have to defend myself, and with my current state, I wasn't sure there would be much defending. I should have known the only use I'd be was as bait. I shifted the spear. Desperately trying to give me some chance of surviving this. I could barely lift it. Not that the nausea I was feeling would help me move at all. I could only hope that the people scattered through the trees would try to keep me safe. They wouldn't watch as someone was innocently slaughtered, would they?

I wasn't waiting long on my own. I hefted the

spear against my side, making sure the sharper end was facing out. It felt unwieldy but it was my only shot. If I was lucky, I might get a few hits at it. It could slow it down or distract it enough for me to find somewhere to run. I was faced with the same problem as before, where would I run to. Would the people from the camp let me run anyway? I felt trapped and angry. It was nice to know they were willing to sacrifice one person to kill one zombie.

All too soon the zombie emerged from the darkness. It lumbered into my clearing. Slowly, carefully making its way towards me. I'd never seen one behave like that before, but I'd also never seen one interact with someone with an open wound. Despite its hesitancy, it was focused. Focused entirely in my direction. As though it could see me.

I took a step back, faltering as my head spun again. I'd manage to survive the past few months without getting too close to one. Now, in the space of two weeks, I'd seen more than I could ever want. At least before, I had the ability to protect myself. With the wound on my arm and the dizziness that plagued my thoughts, I would be lucky to last more than a few minutes.

Its lurching deliberated steps helped me keep the thing in my sights. I said thanks that this one wasn't running. That it couldn't run. Another step back. A branch snapped beneath my foot. I held my breath. The zombie zeroed in on me. It staggered forward as I wedged the spear back against my side, knees bent awaiting the first touch. As it came within reach, I jabbed at its face, glancing off what remained of its chin. The zombie tried to grasp at the weapon, too slow for my pained retreat. I tried not to think of the person this creature had been. I ignored the band t-shirt, now ripped and bloodied, hanging from its frame. This was once someone's son. Did they know what had happened to him? I shook my head to clear the emotions clouding my judgement.

I took another step back and changed the position of the spear. I jabbed again. Again, it stopped and tried to grab it. It wasn't enough to keep me alive, but it might prolong the end I was imagining. I was bait. Bait doesn't get the chance to survive.

I was feeling confident about my chances until a noise caught my attention. The zombie focused on the intrusion. A low rumble emanating from it. Dread filled me. I would struggle to survive against one. Any more and I know that I would never make it out of here alive. I wouldn't know if Rachel and Daniel survived. I wouldn't live to see a cure. It would be over. In this patch of trees and used as bait.

The noise sounded again, this time to my side. It was louder, closer. The zombie in front of me moved towards the new threat. If there was more than one, did that mean Nick had lied to everyone? Or were they not prepared for this one? Neither questioned alleviated the panic rising through me.

My fears were confirmed as a figure stumbled into view. I took a step to the side, attempting to distance myself from both threats. I closed my eyes and prayed. Prayed that they would turn on each other rather than both attack me. I was curious. How they behaved in this moment could give more insight into their overall behaviour. Not that I would be around long enough to do anything with the knowledge.

As the second moved closer, I got a strange feeling from it. There was something off about it. I couldn't figure it out, but it didn't seem right. The first one shuffled closer, trying to guess where it was. The eyesight issue must be a universal thing once a person changed. We had to have one advantage over them. The second one stumbled slightly to its left. The two danced sluggishly along the edge of the trees. No malice or anger, only frustration from the first one on the scene. Emotion, they were showing signs of emotion.

Curiosity rose inside me, urging me to take a step forward and note what the two creatures were doing. Common sense pulled me back a few more steps. My vision moved in and out of focus as I tried to keep an eye on where they were going. Leaves rustled behind me. I froze. Please let that be one of Nick's team. Please don't let it be something else trying to kill me. I repeated over and over in my head.

The zombies barely interacted, but the second one didn't move any closer. It gave up its quarry, me, but it didn't leave from where it stood. Maybe hoping for a scrap of what was left. The first turned back to me, in what I thought was a triumphant manner, and inched closer.

Another noise sounded behind me. I fought the urge to twist round and see what new danger awaited. I gripped the spear in my hand. Letting the coarse bark ground me. Stopping me from spiralling and giving in. I didn't want to panic. I knew I needed to stay calm, focus on surviving this. But you try telling yourself to stay calm in this situation. Again, a noise sounded from behind me. Closing in each time.

"Come on Anna, you've dealt with worse. Deep breaths."

Both zombies stared at me. I almost lost my nerve. I'd never seen any of them stare so intently at anything before. I moved slowly to my left, aiming for the tree line. If I could make it behind some safety, I might make it out of this. If only Nick hadn't cut my arm, my odds of surviving this would be higher. I've never been the fastest runner, but I could have evaded them. Or at least made it out of here with enough chance to survive.

The zombie had decided to follow me. It took maybe four steps when it was hit by something. A guttural, animalistic noise erupted from its mouth. I'd never been happier that something could feel pain. Something else hit it. I stumbled backwards, trying to pull myself to safety when I backed into something. I started to fall forward when I was grabbed by the arm. I stifled the shriek that reverberated in my body. A hand wrapped itself over my mouth as an added precaution.

"Shush Anna, it's us." I heard a familiar voice say.

I almost collapsed into the body behind me. Relief washing through me.

"Follow my steps, don't make too much noise."

I nodded as I was pulled backwards. Away from the two zombies howling in pain. Away from what I thought would be my grave. Once we were sheltered by the trees I turned to face my saviour.

"I can't believe you found me. Why didn't you carry on and leave? You could have been safely away by now."

Rachel peered behind her brother's shoulder. "We

couldn't leave you here. Not after you gave yourself up to save us. It would be like leaving Daniel behind. You're family." She paused. "Almost like the weird distant cousin who you'd hate to lose." Her face broke into the biggest grin.

"Thanks, I feel so touched." I responded, my face mimicking hers.

"Quiet," Daniel said. "We're not sure if they want to keep you here for longer or not, but we need to go while they're distracted with those two."

"Good thinking." I went to move as the world swirled around me again and I stumbled forward.

Daniel caught me, concern quickly flashing over his usually unreadable face. "I hadn't noticed that."

"Yeah, it's my souvenir from a wonderful trip." I said weakly, waiting for the world to right itself. "Do you have anything that can help?"

"I do!" Rachel said.

She rummaged through her bag before pulling out what looked like a cut up sheet and a bottle of vodka.

"Where did you? Never mind, can you help? I don't know if I can manage."

She smiled sheepishly at me. "I thought it might be fun to try, but I never got the chance." She looked at my arm. "This is going to hurt. Danny, grab her hand, we need to make sure she doesn't make a noise."

Daniel grabbed the spear from my left hand as he grasped my palm. "Squeeze as hard as you need to."

I nodded as Rachel poured the liquid over the wound. I clenched my jaw and squeezed until my knuckles turned white. She dabbed at the liquid before wrapping the strips tightly around my arm. The wound pulsated, but it was better than before.

"Let's go and get out of here quick." I plucked the spear from Daniel's hand.

Daniel took the lead and picked his way through the trees. There was a mess of roots, bushes, plants, and rubble but he seemed to know where he was going. The trees were starting to thin when I heard a noise behind us.

"Rachel, go in front of me. I'll make sure nothing's behind us."

"Are you sure?" Her eyes peered at me, full of concern.

"Go," I said pushing her forward.

She followed her brother's path. I hesitated. I knew someone or something was behind us. I took a quick look over my shoulder before trailing behind the twins. Then I felt it. A searing hot pain flashed through my leg. If I'd not had the spear, I'd have fallen. I bit my cheek to stop the scream that wanted to fight its way through my body.

I didn't have time to stop and see how bad it was. I pushed forward, ignoring the throbbing.

"Please have missed an artery. Please have missed an artery." I mumbled to myself. A mantra of hope that I might survive this. I could see Rachel and Daniel weaving their way through the trees in front of me. They hadn't heard what had happened, and they were getting further away. I let them go. If they didn't get out of this because of me, I'd never forgive myself. Which would be easy if my projected lifespan of a few minutes was right.

I pushed myself forward. Listening for any sound of pursuit. Whoever had done this had vanished. Maybe a bullet to the leg was enough payback. I braced myself as I dropped to my knees. My knuckles turned white as they gripped the spear for support. My eyes watered, and I choked back a sob as I started to pull myself across the floor. If I was lucky, I'd be able to find somewhere to crawl under. I might even find something in my own bag to clean out my leg.

The only good thing from this was my arm no longer felt like it was hurting.

Day 38

I wrote as much as I could yesterday. I didn't want to forget anything, but I wasn't in the best place. Even now the world seems fuzzier. Too much blood has left my body in the past 24 hours. Between my leg and my arm, I'm surprised I woke up this morning. One more day to live. If this is a life worth living anymore.

I managed to scrap some branches around me and keep most of the cold and the rain out. It was only a temporary hideout, but I felt safer. Plus, there was no way anyone would think this was constructed. There were barely enough branches to cover me. I was lucky it's been dark. No one could mistake the mass under the broken limbs as a person. The only downside to this is I've lost Rachel and Daniel again. When they came back for me. Maybe it's better this way.

My leg is in agony. I think whatever I was hit with is still lodged there. At least it feels like it. I've only been able to see one hole in my leg which isn't giving me a lot of hope. I tried to clean it out as best I could last night and ripped apart one of the cleaner shirts from my bag. That should at least stop much else from getting in it. I tried to make a tourniquet, but I don't think it's tight enough to completely stop the bleeding. My saving grace is my artery seems to be fine. At least I woke up this morning, so I'm guessing it is.

My arm is feeling better. I unwound part of the makeshift bandage and it looks like the two pieces are gluing themselves back together. At least I'll only have to deal with one life-threatening injury.

Day 39

My new goal is to: one survive, and two find Rachel and Daniel. I might not be much use anymore, but I need to know they're safe. And if it comes to the worst of it, they will be able to take my things to keep going for a little longer.

My movements have slowed down. I can barely walk and without the spear I was given, I don't think I'd have been able to at all. My leg is aching. The wound isn't healing. I'm getting used to the dull throbbing in my thigh. Maybe if I can pull myself together, I'll be able to make up some ground and find where Daniel might have led Rachel. Maybe.

I need to find somewhere for me to go that's safe. Somewhere with a doctor, or a surgeon. Anyone who might be able to save my leg. Save my life. A best-case scenario for sure. Also, the most unlikely option. Would there be any doctors left? There was so much confusion when this happened at the start. The first wave of casualties went to their doctors and their hospitals. No one knew what was happening until it was too late. I'd be amazed if there were any medical professionals left. If they are, I can't imagine I'll stumble into one. I'm not that lucky.

The best hope I have is for my leg to heal. I might limp for the rest of my life, but at least I'd be alive. That's all I want.

Day 40

I can't get out from these trees!

I feel like I'm being trapped, held back from any escape. I'm lost. I'm exhausted. I can barely think straight from the pain that's constantly plaguing me. Every step feels like fire in my leg. My arm is itching, which I'm taking as a good sign, but it's still there. When I want to sleep, there's no end to it. I don't know if the wounds will kill me off, or the sleep exhaustion.

The realisation that time is running out has started to take root. It's weird. You always know you're going to die, but it never seems obvious until you can feel its cold grasp reaching out for you. I can feel the icy tendrils reaching out, wrapping around my limbs. Gently pulling me closer to the abyss.

I swapped the material over on my leg this morning. It doesn't look good. I'm itching to rinse it out with scalding water. Sure, fire doesn't attract zombies, but I don't want to attract anything else to me either. If I can pick up my pace, I might be able to find somewhere safe to clean it out.

I should be panicking more. I shouldn't be so willing to let go. I'm worried if I give up all hope, even the hope of only being able to clean it out, then I'll have given up on living. Losing any hope won't end well for me. Despite my current situation I'm going to keep going. I need to put one foot in front of the other until I literally can't move any longer.

Days 41 and 42

Yesterday was bad. Really bad. The pain in my leg worsened to the point where I couldn't stand on it. I curled up under some branches. Two days I've spent curled up in the same place. I've barely eaten. I want to move. I need to move, but I can't shake the pain. I rummaged through my bag, looking for anything that might help me. Anything to take the edge off. When I found it. The holy grail. A packet of paracetamol had fallen into one of the crevices at the bottom of my bag. I'm hoping that once they settle and pull apart some of the pain, I'll be able to set off again.

I'm hoping tomorrow will be the day I can pull myself from the trees' shadow. Without this injury, I would have been free of it days ago. I'm worried I will need the sort of energy non-injured Anna had. My weakened, limping state might not be enough to get me out. The dark cloud is threatening to settle on me, but I will be positive. Even a few more steps means that I've survived to another day.

Tomorrow, I have to move. If I don't, I might never get out of here. The noises of the trees are making me jump. It's been another two days of little sleep. Every time I settle down, something happens. The pain shoots through my leg or something twitches nearby, breaking my rest. I need to move, for my own sanity if nothing else.

Day 43

I managed it! I moved from my pit of despair. I'm not sure how far I've gone, but I got out of there. I'm not sure if I've made any sort of significant progress to escaping from the psychopaths around here. But I moved. That's all that matters. My leg ached and grumbled every step of the way, but at least I don't have to worry about slowly becoming a part of the undergrowth.

Even such a small accomplishment has me feeling optimistic. With the happiness I'm feeling now, I can see myself getting out of this alive. I might even manage to find a safe place to stay until all this is dealt with. I'm feeling more and more optimistic I'll be able to find Rachel and Daniel as well. If I can keep moving forwards, I shouldn't have any issues with stumbling across them. I think it's been nearly a week, I'm not sure if I'm counting my days right. But they can't have gone on without looking for me, right? They came back for me.

As long as I can find enough food to keep me going, I will find them. I've barely eaten these past few days, but my bag is getting lighter. Maybe they will have some food to spare. I'd be willing to take anything if it meant I'd found them again.

Day 44

I found them. Two days of positivity is enough to get anyone thinking they can survive an apocalypse. But I did it. I stumbled across a small hut. I'm not sure what it used to be. It was run down and ruined, but I thought it could have something inside to help keep me going. I peered inside, and they were about to leave. I've never considered myself a lucky person, and with some of what's happened, I still don't. But I wasn't going to question this.

"Rachel. Daniel." I called out.

They both quickly turned around to see me frantically waving at them from a small window. Their faces lit up. I don't think there were any three people happier than us at that moment. I couldn't help myself; my face broke out into the biggest smile I'd given in months.

"Anna, you found us!" Rachel exclaimed.

She grabbed her bag and ran out of the building. Tears slipped from her eyes as she pulled me to her.

"I didn't think I'd be able to manage it, but I have. I can't believe you were here."

"We'd gone further, but after a couple of days without you catching up, I persuaded Daniel to turn back. I wanted to know you were okay. I knew you'd find us. I knew you wouldn't leave us behind." She laughed and sobbed at the same time. Palming the streaks left on her face.

"Nope, not left behind. I did let you go without me. I didn't want to slow you down." I gestured to my makeshift walking stick and the wrapping around my leg. "I got hit. Not long after I pushed you in front of me. I didn't think I was going to make it and I didn't want to risk your chance of surviving. I've struggled to move, but it's slowly getting better."

"What's getting better?" Daniel asked as he caught up to us.

I was about to answer when he looked at my leg. His face dropped. It was a quick reaction. He tried to hide it before either of us could tell that he was worried. It made me feel like I was right to have worried about this.

"Bullet wound," I said. "Or at least I think it is. There's no exit wound so I'm not sure what's lodged there. If it is, it must be the only gun they have. No idea where they picked it up from, not that we should be worrying about that." I looked at the concern etched on both faces. "Don't worry, I'm not as fast as I used to be, but I can move. That's all that matters. I've managed to drag myself this far."

"I guess so." Daniel said eyebrows furrowed as he stared at my leg. "Are you sure you can walk?"

"I made it here, didn't I? I can soldier on."

He nodded his head, but he didn't look convinced.

"It's okay, Anna. I'll give you a hand where needed." Rachel smiled at me. "We can't leave you behind. Also, we kept hold of this for you." She held out my cricket bat. I wiped at the wet streaks on my face.

They kept their pace slow for me, and Rachel helped with any of the more difficult bits of terrain. I knew I was slowing them down, but selfishly I didn't care. I needed to be travelling with someone. I was happy it was these two someones I was travelling with again. They might help me keep hold of this positive feeling.

Days 45 and 46

I've been trying to keep track of the days, but my head hasn't been feeling great. I may have lost a few along the way, but from what I can remember today is 46 days since I started this little diary. I've not been able to keep my thoughts straight over the past few days. Certain things are starting to merge into one. We've been moving forward, but I can't remember much that has happened.

I'm blacking out. There are holes in my memories. I can't remember how we're getting from one place to another. Maybe this is my body's way of healing. Now I have two people to help me.

I've been trying to concentrate on moving. Making sure that one foot is still going in front of the other. I had thought the pain in my leg was getting better, but the throbbing has come back now. I've been ignoring it. Pretending it's not there. I rebandaged it a few days ago and it seemed fine, but I've still not been able to clean it out fully. I'm hoping we can find a house with running water soon. The last one we stopped in, it wouldn't work. I don't know what was wrong. A house with working taps, that's all I'm hoping for now.

Day 47

We're still going forward. My spirits have been lifted since I'm back with other people. It doesn't seem as though anyone is following us. With our slow pace, we should have spotted anyone by now. We've listened out for anything unusual but only my laboured breathing is out of the ordinary.

"Does, no wait." Rachel said unhooking herself from my arm. "Does that look like some houses down there?"

I pulled my head up from staring at the ground. I squinted in her direction, but I couldn't make anything out. We'd been weaving along the edge of a road and trees for the past day.

"I can't tell, Rach. It looks like you might be right, though." Daniel said.

He was already in front of us by a few steps, but he jogged further ahead.

"Yeah, looks like we're finally going to be able to find some walls to surround us." He called over his shoulder.

"D'you think you'll be able to reach it?" Rachel asked me, watching as I struggled to breathe.

"I'll be fine." I smiled weakly at her. "Go on ahead, I'll catch up. I might be a little slower now, but I can get there. Especially if there are walls and something nice to sleep on."

She smiled back at me, before turning to follow her brother. As soon as she turned, I allowed a small grimace to cross my face. I'd been holding in more pain than I thought. I made a mental note to retie the bandage around my leg. The throbbing had started up again, along with the shooting pains. If I could tighten the wrapping, it might take some of the pain off.

I gripped my makeshift walking stick and willed myself to walk a little quicker. I didn't slow their pace too much, but I didn't want them to worry more than they already were. The feeling of my leg splintering increased with each step I took. A noise sounded from behind me. I stumbled as I tried to spin. I was more on edge now. Being injured and weak was causing my anxiety to run on overdrive. Would I be able to outrun anything if it came for me?

I pushed myself on and in less time than I thought, I had caught up to them. I know the real reason is they don't want to lose me again. It was sweet but didn't make me feel much better.

"I knew we would find something! I told you I could see something." Rachel beamed at me as I staggered the last few steps. "Hopefully, there will be someone there who can help you."

As much as I wanted to give into her optimism, my sense of realism wouldn't let me. If anyone was there, it would be a miracle. Who would stick around in this? It's not like we have houses that can keep out a horde of zombies trying to eat you. No, anyone who lived there would be long gone. As much as I thought it, I couldn't say it to Rachel. She looked so hopeful and happy. It's not something I wanted to wreck.

"You might be being too positive, Rach. It's unlikely anyone has stuck around." Daniel said.

"Well, even if no one stuck around you don't know that other people haven't turned up here. You've got to have a little faith, Dan. If not, what's the point?" She turned to him, "I know I'm being naive, but I can't give up. If I give up now, why should I even try to survive this?"

It was the first time I'd seen Rachel's optimism slip. I understood her completely. It's one of the reasons I've not totally given in. If I had, I may as well not have tried to find them again. I could have stayed curled up in a ball waiting for someone or something to finish me off. Maybe we were all trying to force optimism on the other. Daniel looked shocked at her outburst. He'd not noticed the entire world turning upside down had affected her this much.

"Well, we'll never know if we don't go and check out the place. Daniel, would you mind scouting it out? I would, but I'm not so sure I'm as silent as I used to be." I gestured to my poorly bandaged leg.

He smiled at me. "Sure Anna, I'll go check it out. Wait here, and I'll come back for you both."

"I'm sure we'll find someone to help you. We won't give up hope for you." Rachel said as we watched him walk towards the houses.

"Thanks, Rachel. If we're lucky, we might stumble

across them sooner rather than later."

"I'm gonna stay positive for the both of us." She moved closer to me, wrapping her arm around my shoulders.

My eyes prickled at the gesture. How had I stumbled across these people? They let me help them, and they were willing to risk themselves to help me. We all looked out for each other. I couldn't imagine us not being together in this crazy adventure.

I leaned myself against a fence post. Even with the spear as an aid, I couldn't stand up for too long without support. I didn't know how long it would take for Daniel to scout the place, but I couldn't imagine that he wouldn't be 100% sure it was safe before he brought us down. I don't think he would forgive himself if something was hiding in a cupboard, and it killed us all. Rachel looked like she was trying to keep watch for anything, but she didn't seem to be fully focused.

From her earlier outbreak, I knew she wasn't unaware of the dangers, but it didn't make it easy to stay switched on all the time. Watching her fiddle with the barren branches of a nearby tree I realised how young they both were. To have gone through all this, not knowing if life would ever be safe again? They were handling it better than I would have at the same age. It's not easy to keep yourself strong. Anyone can lapse back when they feel safe enough. I wouldn't want that to change though. Everyone needs distractions.

Daniel's return broke my train of thoughts.

"The coast is clear. Unfortunately, there's no one there. But there is a couple of beds, so at least we should be able to rest up." He turned to look at me, "having your leg rested properly should help a little. If only to take the pressure off."

"What are we hanging around here for then?" I grinned. "I need to get me some rest in that bed asap."

I pushed myself from the post, and with small steps, headed the way Daniel had come from. I couldn't wait to lie down on something that wasn't on the ground.

Day 48

It might not have been a memory foam mattress, but last night was the greatest I had slept in ages. I actually woke up feeling rested. Being surrounded by four walls, and with a mattress underneath me, had brought back some of my optimism.

My arm was still painful, but nowhere near as painful as my leg. The last I checked, it had been healing. I wouldn't have the nicest looking arm, but it would be okay. My leg wasn't feeling as bad as it had been doing. Daniel was right, getting the pressure off it and raising it a little had helped. Maybe life wasn't as bad as I thought it was. We could take on anything as long as we were together. Only, maybe there would be more limping than before.

We'd stumbled onto the outer edges of a village. Civilisation was slowly emerging onto the landscape, but we'd stumbled across one of the smaller cottages. It had been abandoned for a while. Especially if the cupboards were anything to go by. They were almost bare. I'm guessing whoever lived here had taken what they could with them and there hadn't been many people passing through. There was the odd selection of out-of-date tinned food, but it would be good enough for us. Anything to help us live another day was worth picking up.

"We should keep going." I said to them both. "It's nice being inside, but we should be able to find somewhere warm and dry to rest now. It might help us to pick up more food as well."

They both nodded at me.

"I'll go ahead and see if I can grab any supplies from any of the houses we pass."

"Okay, no point in all three of us going in each one. Can you check if any painkillers or anything are lying around? We're almost out."

"Sure, should be easy enough to look out for."

"I'm so glad that we've made it back to somewhere with beds every night." Rachel said, her hope shining through.

We grabbed our bags, and any other little things we thought might be useful and headed out. No point in waiting for something to come find us. I hoped we wouldn't go too far past the village before we needed to rest again. I don't know if I could face sleeping in the mud for another night.

Day 49

My leg has ached non-stop today. I'd managed to clean it in the house. Something I don't want to have to do again, but honestly, I think I'll have to. I wound the bandage as tight as I could, but it doesn't seem to have helped. I don't know if this is a good type of pain or not. With the pain I'm feeling, I'm leaning more towards bad. It's been nearly two weeks, or has it been more than two weeks? Whatever, it's been a good while since I was shot, but it doesn't look like the wound is doing any better. The only good thing is the blood isn't oozing out as much. I still think whatever was shot at me is lodged in my leg. That can't be helping it.

I've been keeping the state of it hidden from Rachel and Daniel. At least until I know there is something I can say about it. I don't need them worrying as much as me and maybe there won't be anything to worry about. It does mean I'm struggling to keep up their pace. I was struggling before, but now it's almost unbearable.

"Are you okay, Anna? You don't look too good." Rachel asked.

"I'm fine, my leg is aching a little more than before. I'm sure it's fine. I think the paracetamol has worn off." I replied.

"Okay, if you're sure. But if it gets worse let us know. We might be able to do something to help."

"If I think I can't manage on my own, I will." I smiled.

Daniel didn't say anything to me, but he was staring.

"You alright, Daniel?"

"Yeah, there's nothing wrong with me."

I didn't want to take it to heart, but it felt like he knew I was lying. I didn't want to deceive them, I didn't. I didn't know how to tell them. There wasn't anything they could do to help. Being surrounded by houses and having somewhere dry to sleep was all I needed and without them, I wouldn't be doing that. It was easier to walk out here, no more roots or bits of foliage waiting to trip me up. Waiting to cause me that extra bit of pain. My main issue was I felt more exposed out here. I felt on edge and the light-headedness from the pain wasn't curbing my fear.

We were slowly making our way across the country. I don't know if we had a destination in mind anymore. We weren't travelling as fast as before, thanks to my newly decreased mobility. But every step took us further away from Nick and his horde of zombie killers. Any distance from them was a blessing.

Days 50 and 51

I'm thankful we've been able to stumble across the edge of this village. Or is it a town? I'm not sure. The weather has turned. There's a bite in the air and it feels like tiny needles pricking at our skin as we try to move. Having four walls to keep us warm when we rest is helping, and with the rest, I need now it's been a blessing.

We've been lucky in being able to scavenge some warmer clothes and accessories. Why would you leave these things behind? Hats, scarves, gloves, and jumpers are so useful. Or maybe whoever lived in these houses before had too many? I guess I left all of mine behind as well. There was a blind panic on all of us at the start.

I tried to find time to note this down yesterday, but energy is fleeting when you're trying to heal. I hope I've not missed anything out.

"When we came to find you, we overheard some of those people talking." Daniel said as we arranged all the cushions and blankets into a fort in the living room.

"About?" I prompted.

"I don't know if it's important, but I can't stop thinking over it. I brushed it off, but it might make sense."

"What was it?"

"About how all of this started." He gestured vaguely. "They thought it had been done on purpose. That it was man-made and released on us, but by the people in charge. I can't stop thinking about it. It explains why no one is trying to help, and why the power was cut. It's almost like everyone in charge disappeared. If it wasn't done on purpose, then how would they know to cut the power when they did?"

"They wouldn't have done this to us, Danny. Why would anyone do this to the people they are supposed to look after?" Rachel asked.

"I don't know. But it makes sense."

"Don't let it get to you, Daniel. Even in an apocalypse, there are going to be conspiracy theorists. We reason out worries in ways that make sense to us. Try not to let it bother you."

"You don't get it. I've felt like there was something off about all of this anyway. How it appeared out of nowhere. I can't shake the feeling that this is why. What if this was done on purpose? Why would anyone let this happen to everything?" He looked frantic the more he thought about what he said.

"Look, Daniel, even if our own country has sold us out like this, it doesn't mean there aren't some people trying to help. If it was only our government and politicians, it doesn't mean the entire world has done the same thing."

"But what if they have? What if the entire world

is like this? Is any country the same as before, or have we all been infected with this? We might never get to live a normal life again and it could have been a decision someone made."

"Danny, what did I say the other day?" Rachel asked quietly. Her eyes searching out his. "If we give up hope, we might as well not bother trying. There might be some awful people out there, but we can't say everyone is the same. If there's no way to survive, why are we bothering?"

He let the words sink in. He sighed. "You're right, but it makes me feel helpless. I don't get why we've been left like this if another country is running fine."

I snorted. "Our country has ignored plenty others in its time. Wars, dictatorships, famine, it doesn't surprise me we're on the receiving end. No one wants to deal with something that doesn't directly impact them."

Conspiracy theories had never fascinated me before, but I had to agree with Daniel. If only in this diary. Countless issues threatened our country before this happened. More and more people falling into poverty. No jobs were available to the majority of people. Maybe it was a way to ease the situation, a way to wipe some of the slate clean? Whatever it was, I didn't want to think about the rest of the world having gone in the same direction. Even if other places hadn't done this, was there a way it had been contained?

You try to be positive during an apocalypse, then a thought like this buries itself in your mind. Refusing to let go of the space it occupied, claiming squatter's rights. I wonder how many other people have thought it. Did it make them lose hope, push them over the edge, or did it force them to survive despite this?

Day 52

My leg is not healing. I can barely hide it anymore. Every time I move, I can feel the pain ricocheting through my body. I feel like I'm on fire. I don't think I'm going to survive this. It's been too long with no improvement. Too long with no way to clean it out. It's warm, warmer than any leg should be at this time of year.

I don't know what I'm going to do. How can I tell them?

Day 53

"Are you okay, Anna?" Rachel asked me.

"Yeah, I'm fine." I said through gritted teeth.

"You don't seem fine. You can tell us if something's wrong."

"I know I can." I sighed, struggling to get the words out.

"It's your leg, isn't it?" Daniel said. Not pausing to look at me.

Tears rose to my eyes, my nose prickled. "Yeah, just my leg." I wiped the water from my eyes. "My arm's fine, scarred but fine. My leg, I don't know if it can be fixed." I sighed, pausing in our walk. "I think it's infected, I think it's been infected for days. The last time I cleaned it out was not pretty. I thought it was getting better." I laughed bitterly, "but I think I was deluding myself. I needed a doctor, or at least clean water when it first happened."

"D'you think you'll be okay?" Rachel asked quietly, eyes shining with emotion.

"I don't know. No, maybe. Look, I didn't want to say anything because I didn't know what would happen. I didn't want to worry you guys."

"You could have said something, Anna. Anything. We might have been more worried if we woke up to you dead, or worse a zombie."

"You're right, Daniel. It was selfish of me. I've not been thinking straight. I hoped we'd find a house with some antibiotics that had been left behind, or a pharmacy that hadn't been ransacked. Something that might help. But it doesn't look like that's going to happen."

"At least we can all keep a lookout for these now." He said, looking intently at me. "Are you sure your arm is fine?"

"Yeah, I've not bandaged it for ages. Like I said it's scarred but healed."

Rachel looked crestfallen. I knew she would. "I wish you'd told us sooner. Me and Daniel could have been scouting out quicker to see if there was anything to help you."

"I've done it in every house we stopped at."

"But we could have been looking in the ones that we've been walking past. We'll have to start now."

She was right, they both were. If I had mentioned this sooner, they could have been helping along the way. Now, I felt like I was limping against the clock.

Daniel veered off our path and headed towards the nearest house. Maybe my luck wouldn't run out now. Rachel slowed her pace, letting me set the speed. I was grateful for it. Not having to force myself to move quicker had a positive effect on me. At least it stopped the fatigue which threatened to overwhelm me each day. The pain in my leg didn't lessen, but I didn't feel it getting worse.

148

Days 54, 55, and 56

I don't want to keep repeating myself. And the past few days would be repeated. No matter how many houses Rachel or Daniel break into, they haven't been able to find any antibiotics. They've come back with a lot of pain killers which has helped me travel, but it's only temporary relief. There was a pharmacy, but we couldn't find anything. I joked about taking the morphine and they could leave me behind, but they both glared at me.

My leg is in constant pain, and my optimism was draining. Sometimes this diary is a good way to get my thoughts out, help free up some space in my mind. Other times, I feel like it's mocking me. I know it can't, not really. But making myself write down the worst of it doesn't help lighten the mood.

We've rested for longer today. I can barely stand when the tablets wear off. I've been taking more and more each day, not something I think I can do for much longer. We set up camp in a nice little semi-detached with a garden, not that we are making much use of it. Daniel has been searching through the neighbourhood while Rachel lets me sleep.

Rachel was hopeful something would turn up for us. That it would only be a matter of time before we stumbled across something that would save my leg. That would save me. I didn't dissuade her. I would love for them to find a way to cure my leg, to get rid of this infection. To have the chance to walk around without bracing for pain with every step. Not having to feel a bandage become sodden with liquid and whatever else was weeping from the wound.

Honestly, I would let them search for as long as they wanted to. It would mean I could stay cosied in this bed, in this house, and not have to worry about moving.

Day 57

Daniel came back from his search not long ago. He'd managed to find more food for us, but nothing for my leg. A mounting pile of ibuprofen laid next to me on the bedside table, so not all bad news. No cure, but also no pain. There weren't many tablets left in the packets, but it was enough.

"How's the leg holding up?" He asked me.

"Bad." I laughed weakly. "It doesn't feel as bad as it was, but I've not moved much which has to help. The infection's still there."

"Anything helping it?"

I shook my head. "Cleaning it helps a little. The best we can do unless we can find anything to cure it."

"Hopefully, we'll find something." He squeezed my arm through the duvet. "Sorry I've not been able to find anything so far. Want me to warm up some water?"

"S'not your fault. If there aren't any, there aren't any. You can't do anything about that. Warm water will help though. I can try and psyche myself out of bed then."

Daniel left me. I know I said hot water might work, but I didn't hold much hope for it. My leg was feeling better today. A bed to yourself was the cure to all life's woes. I'd not moved much since we got here. I have no idea what any of the other rooms look like. I crawled into the first bed I saw and hadn't been able to move myself since.

I chucked my grubby clothes on the floor and pulled on a fresh t-shirt and jogging bottoms from one of the drawers. They were oversized, but I needed the comfort. Fresh clothes were a luxury I never knew I'd miss. Before I changed, I brought the bowl of steaming water into my room to change my bandage. Despite having done this a few times already, I wasn't prepared for the sight. It was all angry looking and red. The hot water burned through me, hopefully, a good sign, before I rewrapped it with a clean bed sheet I'd found. The good thing about an apocalypse was no one wanted to take their bedding with them.

The colour of the wound was starting to worry me, and the heat that came from it made me uncomfortable.

"Please be wrong." I whispered to myself.

Day 58

Sweat dripped down my face. My hair felt mattered and stuck to the sodden pillow beneath me. Had someone thrown water over me? As much as I wished it was a cruel prank, I knew the truth. My head was in agony, either from the potential dehydration or the fever that burned every inch of my skin. I struggled to open my eyes. The world spinning as soon as I did. Maybe I should have paid more attention to my leg than I had been doing.

My chances of survival were slowly slipping by. Rachel and Daniel needed to know. There were no words to soften the blow, but now they would be better off without me. This was the last thing I could do for them.

I forced myself from the bed, t-shirt clinging to my back. I moved sluggishly to the kitchen, the hot knife of pain in my leg worsening with each step. So much for proper rest making me feel better. They were faced away from me as I entered the room. I stood awkwardly by the door, not sure what I wanted, no, what I needed to say. The thought of what I was doing made my nose itch, and my eyes burn. This was not a goodbye any of us wanted. What choice did I have?

The pain was starting to become unbearable. My leg burned through the fabric of the pants I'd put on yesterday. If I felt like I was making the wrong choice, this solidified my position. I'd become a problem. I couldn't let them die because they were keeping me safe.

"I think you two are going to have to go on without me." I eventually managed to say. My voice raspy and unfamiliar to my ears.

Rachel turned to look at me, smiling. "Don't be silly, Anna. We'll make sure you're okay. We're better off as a group than separating."

"I don't think that's the only thing she means, Rach." Daniel said softly as he turned.

He looked agonised. He must have realised my leg wasn't healing how it should either. No one wanted to admit they were going to die, and someone else wouldn't want to break the news to you. It's something you brush off, hoping you won't have to worry about. I'd been ignoring it myself for the past few days. One bullet to the leg and all my previous surviving meant nothing. Even if we did come across someone, I don't think they'd be able to help. Not now.

"Daniel, she'll be okay. We can all get through this. Together."

"Rachel, look at her. Really look at her. She can barely stand where she is. She's dripping with sweat, and she's been in bed all night. She needed a doctor weeks ago. And now," he sighed, looking away from us both. "And now, it's probably too late."

"He's right, Rachel." I tried to fight back the tears. "I've been trying to hide it. I wanted to find a way to get better for you. But the infection isn't going anywhere. I've cleaned it as much as I can." I laughed sadly. "It's not helping anymore. I didn't want to give up. The thought of you two going on your own breaks my heart. If I don't let you go, I'm worried I'll be the death of you both."

"Don't say that, Anna. We can't lose you as well. Not after everything we've done. Not after everything we've been through." Rachel sobbed, her cheeks glistening with tears.

"I know, but it has to. I can't be the reason you don't make it out of this alive. I'm glad you stumbled into my life. I'm glad you decided to try and steal my food that day." I laughed through the tears. "But now you need to survive. Both of you need to make it out of this alive."

Rachel pushed herself from the table and ran to me, engulfing me in a hug. The tears fell freely as I held her back, her body shaking under my arms. I didn't want to let go. I'd struggle on my own, but I couldn't be their downfall. I couldn't let them see me die. They shouldn't have to see that. They shouldn't have to stop me from becoming another undead. This was the only way I knew they'd be safe from me.

"Daniel, I don't think I'll need the majority of my stuff. Will you help me split it out for you two?"

He nodded solemnly. He knew I was giving up, and he knew there was no talking me out of it. I kept back a couple of things, enough to last me a few days. Maybe longer if I struggled to eat. Everything else I gave to them. Even what was left of my first aid kit. There was nothing in there to help me. I almost gave them my diary. Almost. I hid it down under a shirt. I might need something to keep me sane over the next couple of days.

Daniel split the items into two piles so they could carry them with ease. It didn't look like a lot, but they should be able to find more. It might not be the best, but it would keep them going.

"I'm not delaying you two any further. You need to go. Don't forget to rest, and keep your food topped up." I pulled them both into a hug, my arms tight around their shoulders. "Live." I whispered. "For me. Promise me you will. I know you'll be able to survive this, especially without me holding you back."

Rachel sobbed into my shoulder. "Please don't do this, Anna. How can we leave you behind to die? We'll find someone to help you and come back for you."

I stroked her hair, trying to calm her. "You can leave me behind because it's what you need to do. I'm too far gone. My fever was the last straw. If none of the tablets have helped by now, nothing will. I needed a doctor when it happened. Sure, my leg could be amputated but there's no guarantee that wouldn't become infected. Plus, can you imagine trying to run from a zombie with crutches?"

That made them both laugh, but the mood stayed sombre. I knew this would be difficult, but I didn't realise how difficult it would be.

"Daniel, can you make sure she's okay?"

He pulled me closer. "Of course I will. I'm her big brother. I wish it wasn't ending like this."

"Me too, but you should go soon." I pulled back

from them both, hands fanning under my eyes to remove the remaining tears threatening to spill. "Don't leave it too long. Who knows, maybe I'll survive this, and I'll see you later." I managed a weak smile at them.

"Yeah maybe," he said as he moved to grab his bag. "Come on, Rach, we should go."

"But I don't want to. I can't leave her here."

"You can, and you will." I smiled at her. "Who else will tell people how I bludgeoned a zombie to death then threw up?" I laughed slightly. "Speaking of," I moved to where my bag was left, untying the cricket bat. "I'm not going to need this anymore. Take it." I thrust it into Rachel's unwelcoming hands.

Daniel grabbed hold of her arm and started to pull her away. He grabbed her bag and slung it over his shoulder.

"Come on, we need to go. We might as well make use of some time without rain."

She reluctantly turned and followed after him. I watched as they walked out of the house, letting the tears flow freely down my face. I knew I'd never see them again, but at least they had more of a chance now. At least I wouldn't be the reason for them to not survive. If only I could find a way to survive, but I'm already too far gone.

Days 59, 60, and 61

With no one to keep watch over me, I've let the past few days slip by as I drifted in and out of consciousness. I've not left the house we'd camped in. I can't find the energy to go anywhere else. Not eating isn't helping with this. My appetite went the same time as Rachel and Daniel did. What's the point in eating if you aren't going to survive?

I wanted to be optimistic. I wanted this diary to be optimistic, but I should have known better. A small part of me is clinging to the hope that I'll get out of this alive. I don't know how. I pulled the bandage off last night. I almost threw up at what greeted me. I tried to wipe away as much of the yellow gunk as I could before wrapping more bedsheet around it. My situation is hopeless.

I woke up today listening to the raggedness of my breathing. When that happened, I couldn't say. It was another sign of my growing weakness. I wanted it over sooner rather than later. I felt nauseous waiting for it to happen. How would it end? When would it end? Were Rachel and Daniel still alive? My thoughts circled on those few questions. Returning every time, I let my guard down.

I wasn't ready to say goodbye to them, to myself, to the world. Death is slowly making its way towards me. One agonisingly slow second at a time, but it's coming. A sudden thought hit me, I'd never seen my mum and brother again. I'd not thought of them for so long, and now I'd never know if they'd been looking for me. If they'd survive. The tears and grief threatened to overwhelm me. I couldn't dwell. It wouldn't help me, nothing would.

I'd never been a religious person, but I was hoping there was some sort of afterlife. At least then I'd be able to see everyone again. It might be the only bit of optimism I can summon, but I'll take what I can get.

Days 62, 63, and 64

I moved to one of the other houses. I needed a change of scenery. There was a bed, but I didn't check out the rest of the house. There could be zombies living in one of the other rooms for all I know. But I needed this. A place I hadn't been with them. It stopped the feelings from coming back.

I've not been able to do much, I can't remember what's real and what's not anymore. I can't feel the pain in my leg, but I'm struggling to feel much of anything. There's a wrongness around it. When I try and concentrate on it, I lose focus. My head seems to constantly be covered in sweat. I'm used to small droplets running through my hair and down my cheeks. It doesn't take away any of the heat.

I've been flicking through the diary. Trying to see any signs that I could have done something different. That my path didn't have to end up here. I wouldn't change a thing. Although maybe more washing would have been nice. It breaks me from the reality I'm living. The numbness and fever soon bring me crashing back down to reality. The cold, hard reality I'm living in. I've kept going for this long, that's got to count for something right?

I don't know how much more of this I can face. I don't know how much more I can record. This has been my only constant for so long. It's given me a purpose, something to do. Now, I feel like I'm being mocked. I'll be gone soon, and this diary will still be here. It's not helping me as much as it used to. It was almost like I was writing this for everyone, but with the hope of seeing its impact.

But now? I'll be lucky to live out the week. I won't even know if anyone reads this, if anyone tries to understand what we've been through. Will all these words have been for nothing? The thought depresses me more than I'd like to admit. But it's true. If I leave you here, will anyone find you? Will anyone find me? It might be the only option I have left.

Classified Dossier

Property of United Nation Officials

Report Language: English

Artefact #299

Description: Diary of Anna Louise Smith. Real-life writings during the extended trial of the Zed Flu virus.

This diary is Artefact number 299 out of 5315 as part of the investigations held against the United Kingdom and her government. For a full list of evidence and artefacts retrieved, please consult the United Nations Library for digital records.

Dossier Report

The diary of Anna Louise Smith was found in Birdwood. The condition of this artefact implied it had been left for some time. A full sweep was done within a two square mile radius to determine if any other artefacts could be found. This search proved to be unsuccessful. The conclusion being no one else had left anything of value in this area to analyse as part of the ongoing investigations against the United Kingdom and her associates.

This diary has been carefully analysed by our experts to piece together the effects of the Zed Flu virus experiment in the field. Although there has been little insight from this particular document, we have been able to understand the widespread fear prevalent through this time. The virus was constructed to be passed via contact and was released without any consent from the United Kingdom subjects, or the rest of the world.

Our investigations have provided insight for this virus. This worked in a similar fashion to a parasite once access was gained to the victim's blood stream. The test subjects, or initial victims, experienced significant mutations that removed all humanity and created a need to consume human flesh. This pushed the virus to spread much faster than lab trials had predicted. All attempts to cure those afflicted with the Zed Flu strain have been unsuccessful. This report finds the treatment of these citizens inhumane and contravenes the United Nations meaning of the sanctity of life.

This diary is one of many found during this trial period and shows chaos and confusion in all parts of the island. The controlled experiment brought forward by BioGen Labs Inc, the creators, and the United Kingdom government has proven to be ineffective in their hypothesised outcomes.

Major public figures were evacuated from the island nation prior to the first doses being administered, but only after a cure had been synthesised and distributed to those deemed worthy. Extensive notes and test results were seized from BioGen Labs Inc over the course of this investigation. This further condemns the experiment, and those who authorised it, as it was clear from the tests the extent to which this virus could run if left unsupervised.

This trial resulted in mass homicide, by those afflicted and by those who had not been. The survivors from this experiment are likely to have lasting trauma from the six-month long event. The level of hysteria and panic was ignored by both parties involved, and it was not until contamination spread beyond the national borders that an intervention was made. Due to the secrecy of this experiment, there were no warnings in place to stop people from entering the country. Although air travel was stopped, some were able to land, and contact was made via a fishing boat landing. All ports were sealed once this was revealed.

Once world leaders were able to

establish the framework of isolation, the contamination was stopped from reaching all areas of the globe. The investigation can conclude all traces of this contaminant spread have now been stopped with no new global cases reported over the past four years.

The investigation was concluded five years after the start of this epidemic, and four and half years after the United Nations stepped in to resolve the issue. The United Kingdom has remained closed off from the rest of the world during this time. In part, this has been for the safety of the global citizens as well as to observe for any further mutations. At the writing of this report, no further mutations have been identified.

The ingredients, and process needed, to produce this cure was obtained from BioGen Labs Inc as part of the ongoing investigation and asset seizure. Once batches of the cure were created, armed response teams were landed within the country to distribute to any remaining survivors. Periodic food drop offs have since been made to ensure survival for those left on the island.

Acknowledgments

I almost feel as though this is an award speech. I want to thank my mum for telling me when my writing was boring and pushing me to improve. I've limited my usage of 'overly' in this book. I want to thank my friends for having confidence in me and cheering me on. You might not realise it, but those kind words helped me push through. Thanks to Xee and Cat for helping me decide on the final title. I don't know if I would have been able to decide on my own. Lastly, I want to thank Todd. Without your love of apocalypse fiction, and zombies, I might never have decided to write this. Also, without your prodding this may have stayed a book in progress, never ready to see the world.

About the Author

L.A Binley is a science fiction and fantasy writer. She has a BA Hons in French and Spanish from Bangor University in North Wales. Although it was mainly as an excuse to travel, she believes it has helped with her grammar. Editors are still to be convinced.

When not withering away in front of her computer, she likes to practice her French and Spanish through the medium of song.

To find out more about L.A Binley head to her website below:

https://labinley.com

Join My Newsletter

Want to hear more from me? Head to https://labinley.com/newsletter to sign up to my monthly newsletter. Including sneak peaks for any future projects!

Thanks for reading!
Please add a short review to the store you bought it from,
Or Goodreads, or Storygraph